THE SECRETS OF STAR WHALES

REBECCA THORNE

THE SECRETS
OF
STAR WHALES

REBECCA THORNE

JOLLY FiSH PRESS

Mendota Heights, Minnesota

First Edition
First Printing, 2021

Book design by Jake Nordby
Cover design by Sarah Taplin
Cover illustration by Rebecca Willoway

Jolly Fish Press, an imprint of North Star Editions, Inc.

This is a work of fiction. Names, characters, places, and incidents are either the product of the author's imagination or are used fictitiously, and any resemblance to actual persons living or dead, business establishments, events, or locales is entirely coincidental.

Library of Congress Cataloging-in-Publication Data (pending)
978-1-63163-441-3

Jolly Fish Press
North Star Editions, Inc.
2297 Waters Drive
Mendota Heights, MN 55120
www.jollyfishpress.com

Printed in Canada

To my parents, who always had a book in hand, who challenged me every day to be better. And to my sister, who tried to write a book first and ignited my competitive side. I wouldn't be anywhere without you guys. Thank you. Also, Paige? I win.

1

THE TOURIST FROM THE ABYSS

India twirled the marble-like ball between her fingers, shooting me a wicked grin. "Get ready, Max. You have fifteen seconds."

The education level's tubelike corridor was crowded, and not just with our classmates. The entirety of Azura's students, kids ranging from five to sixteen, were returning from lunch. Well, "returning" would imply that we were going to our respective classrooms, but almost everyone had their noses pressed against the plastiglass windows instead.

Because, in the gaping space beyond, backlit by the bright-pink Kialoa Nebula, a foreign starship was being towed to our space station.

Behind us, Mrs. Smith—our temporary teacher, after Mr. Bruska had his . . . accident—barked, "Back inside, all of you! That idiot's broken ship won't help you on next week's exam. Move!"

"Now or never, Max," India whispered, presenting the tiny ball again. Blue and white swirls wrapped about the orb, and when thrown, it would release a fog so thick I'd have no trouble escaping Mrs. Smith's scrutinizing gaze. "Get this gossip. It's all you."

Now she was just being dramatic. "We don't even need the smoke bomb. Why don't we just sneak out—"

"Too late!" With a wild laugh, she threw it against the polished faux-wood floor. The smoke bomb exploded in a burst of white fog, filling the hallway with coughs and screams. I tried to grab her arm, take her with me, but she shouted, "Tell my stoooory," and vanished in the pandemonium.

"India!"

She was gone. And really, we couldn't waste a good smoke bomb, could we? I sprinted past the other classrooms, ducking into the first adjacent hallway. The potted ficuses provided excellent cover from the teachers thundering toward our classroom—and the chaos.

Azura, our space station, was shaped like a big, multistory wheel. The outer tube rotated to maintain gravity, and spoke-like corridors led to a few elevators in the center. We were on the education level now, but the starship would be docking three stories above, in the hangar level.

I pressed the button to summon one of the elevators and plotted an excuse for why I wasn't in class, just in case the lift was already occupied. But the double doors dinged open without a soul in sight. Airtight! I grinned and bounced inside. All this sneaking around made me feel like . . . like a secret space agent or something.

Jeez, I'd be such a great space agent.

It took a few minutes to arrive at my destination, but I'd already crafted an excuse if confronted: our class was "learning about starship docking protocols," and Mom was supposed to make a presentation. Considering she was the lead harbormaster, everyone on Azura knew her authority. And, of course, I'd be the one sent to retrieve her.

It was foolproof.

Right up until I heard Mom's voice at the end of the corridor.

My excuse only worked with someone who wasn't her. She'd pin me in a second. I swallowed hard, sweat beading on my forehead as I hunted for cover. But this wasn't like the education level. There were no conveniently placed plants to hide behind. I spun, but the elevator was already gone; another would take too long.

Time ticking, I pressed against the smooth wall, which was painted a cheery shade of purple and lined with flickering holographic images of asteroid mining missions from Azura's early years. A vintage e-poster at my side advertised, *Digits Are Yours for the Taking on the Edge of Space! Mine anemonium for a year, live like a king forever*, with a picture of a silvery anemonium asteroid gleaming amid the normal rock. It was all propaganda, but it had propelled Azura into a bustling town . . . at least until the anemonium supply began to dwindle half a century ago.

Now the only people left were the ones who actually *liked* living here. And, occasionally, a real, actual tourist. I pressed myself flatter against the e-poster and tried not to move. Maybe Mom wouldn't notice me.

Standing alone.

In an empty corridor.

Ugh, India and I did *not* think this through.

But Mom was chatting with Kaito, the space traffic controller. I inhaled as they stepped into view, but they were walking with purpose along the outer ring of this level and didn't glance left to see me.

It worked!

Plus, they saved me the time of checking every hangar for my target. I crept to the outer circle, peeked around the corner, and watched them disappear into Hangar 42. The doors slid shut, and silence fell.

I counted to ten, then crept to the hangar. It was sealed tight—standard protocol for welcoming a foreign starship. Not that that'd stop me. My heart pounded as I knelt beside the tiny metal panel just left of the doors, plucking my hydrodriver out of my back pocket. The panel popped off with barely a nudge of the thin tool, revealing a snarl of wires inside.

And past them, the switch to override the locking mechanism.

In my head, a theme song for my escapades was already forming, a litany of swells and staggers that made me feel like I was the lead in an action holovid. I nudged the wires aside— *carefully, carefully*—to reveal the tiny black switch. I moved to press it . . .

And the doors slid open to reveal Mom, waiting with crossed arms.

I screamed.

Wait, wait. *Ahem.* I didn't scream. Screaming was for little kids scared by old stories of flesh-eating sirens in space. No, I merely offered Mom a smirk and a cool two-fingered salute.

Yep. That's what happened.

At some point during my totally legit reaction, I dropped my hydrodriver. The skinny tool skittered across the floor, knocking against Mom's boot. She plucked it off the ground and examined it, as if she'd never seen one before. Which was crazy, considering it could switch between twelve different tools with the flick of a finger; hydrodrivers were a staple in every engineer's toolbox.

But let her look all she wanted. I took advantage of the distraction, subtly reattaching the metal panel in a last-ditch effort to hide my tampering.

It didn't work. The distinct *snap* gained Mom's attention, and with a huff, she shot me *The Look*. You know the one. That stare all moms use, pure derision that silently says, *You messed up*.

I flinched.

"Maxion Cameron Belmont." She drew out my name, forcing me to taste the disappointment in every syllable. "How did I know you'd be here?"

Obviously, someone had seen me sneak away and snitched. With my list of usual suspects from my class—from Nashira Robinson (self-appointed "communicator," AKA gossiper) to Tarynn Zhang (stuffy class president) to Rhett Resnik (holier-than-thou bully)—there were too many possibilities.

But snitching meant giving up the chance to bribe me for juicy gossip . . . and Azurans loved to gossip. That was the real reason India had plucked that smoke bomb from the recesses of her patchwork jacket. Considering we hadn't seen a tourist in three years, a front-row seat to this event would make me *king*.

I mean, *come on.*

But that snarky reply wouldn't win favors with Mom. So I tried something different: my built-in defense these days. "Ah, Mr. Keller asked me to test the integrity of the hangar doors."

A lie, but hopefully a convincing one. Considering my job with Keller was the only thing financing a repair for Dad's decivox, it wasn't so unbelievable. The instrument could still craft a melody, but sitting in a closet for a decade hadn't been kind to it, and sending such a specialized instrument to the inner planets wasn't cheap. But I'd give anything to hear it play properly.

For a breath, my oh-so-convincing lie almost worked. Then Mom rolled her eyes. "Nice try. Mr. Keller wouldn't ask you to work during school hours. Tell me what you're really doing here."

"It's true! You're the one who told me to get a job to 'learn the value of money,'" I said, using air quotes around her words and everything.

Wrong move. She pursed her lips and tapped her foot. "Max."

"Um . . ." With my window closing fast, I switched to classic, shameless begging. Under her Look, I dropped to my knees and clasped my hands together. "Mom, I *have* to get a look at that starship. Please! It was spitting purple exhaust. You know what that means?"

She heaved a sigh. "It means you kids spend too much time at the windows and not enough time studying for your futures."

Yeah, right. We all knew how much studying was getting done now that Mrs. Smith, the infamous teacher of Azura's thirteen-year-olds, had been forced to take on our class of twelve-year-olds as well. Hint: it wasn't much. Especially not with India's smoke bombs.

I cleared my throat and plowed ahead. "Come on, Mom! Purple exhaust? That's only found in a Starkwil generator. Do you know how rare those are? They can cross a star system faster than"—than India could get into trouble, but I wasn't about to say that—"uh, than a miner can clear an asteroid."

There. Perfect for Azura, the has-been mining hub of the Fifth Star System.

Mom glanced over her shoulder. Past her, the hangar's inner airlock doors creaked open with an almost musical trill. Like the first few notes of a symphony, hovering on the precipice of something life changing.

A thrill raced up my spine as a gust of wind from the pressurization process buffeted us, flipping my dark, curly hair into a tizzy. Before Mom could fix it herself, I clawed it back into some semblance of appropriate.

The starship had docked. This was it. I bounced on my toes.

"Just a peek. Please?"

With a sigh, she tossed me the hydrodriver. A slight smile played on her lips. "When you talk like that, you sound just like your father."

Oh. That wasn't my intention. Even the casual mention of Dad closed my throat, choking me. It had been two years since he died, but . . . this was *his* hydrodriver. *He'd* shown me how to override the locking mechanism on Azura's doors. *He'd* taught me about Starkwil generators.

Suddenly, using those things to see a stupid random starship made me cringe. Like I was disrespecting his memory, even though he'd probably be proud of the fact that I could hack a hangar door in half a minute.

Impressed, even.

But Mom's eyes were shiny, which snapped me out of it. I

swallowed past the lump in my throat. It was so hard when Mom cried. I had to be strong for her, so whenever she mentioned Dad, I forced a smile I didn't feel and changed the subject. If we didn't talk about him, she wouldn't cry about him.

And neither would I.

"Camille! Ship's docked. We need you," Kaito bellowed from inside.

Thank the stars for simple distractions. I quickly and carefully compartmentalized my brain, boxing up the emotion around the word "Dad." After two years of practice, I'd gotten pretty darn good at it.

"Be right there." Mom tugged a holopad from her pocket, powering on the thin device with a flick of her wrist. The square, transparent screen glowed gold as it connected to Azura's local network. She studied it for a minute, like she was boxing Dad up in her own mind too.

When she looked at me again, her expression was clear. After a tense moment where I widened my eyes to kicked-puppy levels for the sympathy vote, she ran a hand through her dark hair. "Fine. I'll give you ten minutes. Then it's back to class with you, Maxion, before Mrs. Smith calls again."

*Airtight, i*t worked! On a space station where gossip was the best kind of currency, India and I would be living like royalty for a week. This was *so* worth one of her smoke bombs.

Oblivious to my wicked thoughts, Mom shook her head and strolled back into the docking bay.

I followed like a second shadow, grinning as the foreign starship came into view. This close, I noticed details we hadn't been able to see from the plastiglass windows outside Mrs. Smith's room. The heavy cords one of the miners had attached to the exterior, helping tow it back to Azura. The glowing serial number on the underbelly, registering it with the Department of Galactic Vehicles. And the name, printed in white letters underneath dark cockpit windows: *Calypso.*

I gaped. It was sleek, gorgeous. A Tracker Mark V, maybe a Mark VI—impossible to tell without getting inside the flight deck. But Tracker and Starkwil didn't collaborate on their equipment, which meant this ship was privately modified. My fingers twitched against my hydrodriver, itching to explore, to discover what else its mysterious owner had altered.

"What is *he* doing here?"

A stern voice cut through my awe, and I spun to see Mayor Zhang standing beside Kaito, the space traffic controller. Kaito couldn't care less about me; his watery eyes were glued to the holopad Mom showed him, muttering about the foreign starship as it settled behind us with creaks and pops. His presence made sense. Kaito supervised all open space around Azura, making sure the two-person mineships didn't collide on their way to and from the asteroid belt. Mom, of course, recorded all starship activity. But the mayor?

She had an entire space station to run. She didn't deign to visit just anyone.

I couldn't contain my smirk. This was excellent.

"Camille," Mayor Zhang said, pursing her lips. It was obvious where her daughter Tarynn got her sour attitude. "Shouldn't your son be in class?"

I had to bite down my reply: *Shouldn't you be in your office?* But truthfully, I had no idea what a mayor did during working hours. Maybe she was supposed to be here.

Mom waved off the mayor's concern. "This is an excellent learning opportunity for Max. You know he's going to be an engineer someday, just like his father. The more exposure he gets to new starships, the better for Azura."

Another pang of guilt curdled in my chest, like it always did when Mom insisted I was going to be an engineer. I was good at mechanics, good at starships, but I was good at other things too.

I was good at *music*.

Not that being "good" at music would fix my decivox. Nope. Money talked, and the only digits I had came from working at Mr. Keller's shop. So I let Mom think what she wanted. When I got Dad's decivox back from the inner planets and could amaze her with its true sound, then she'd understand.

Mom flashed me a dazzling smile, and with determination simmering in my soul, I smiled back.

Mayor Zhang sniffed. "Well, Tarynn could learn about diplomacy from this experience, but you don't see me hauling her out of class."

"Maybe you should, if she plans to run for your position when she's older," Mom replied steadily. I shuddered; bossy Tarynn controlling the entirety of Azura? Nothing would make her happier . . . or us more miserable. "Either way, I'm sure Mrs. Smith appreciates the break from so many students."

"Natalia is doing her best. We'll find a substitute for their class soon." Mayor Zhang glanced at me again, pointedly, as if it was my fault our old teacher had broken his leg in five places and had to spend six months at the inner planets for specialized rehabilitation.

If anything, India started that chain of events, not me.

"Job's been posted for three weeks." Mom sighed. "Everyone qualified is busy elsewhere. You know that."

"Ladies," Kaito interrupted, jerking a thumb at the starship. It was fully powered down now, and the seams along the underbelly cracked open. I sucked a breath. The owner was coming out.

"Big smiles, everyone," Mayor Zhang said.

Mom put a hand on my shoulder, and I trembled in anticipation, fingers curling around the hydrodriver. Stars, I wish I had Dad's decivox right now. Something about the worn wooden instrument comforted me a lot more than a cold, hard tool.

The stairs pulled away from the Tracker starship with a hiss and—a cloud of black smoke.

It didn't take an engineer to know *that* wasn't normal.

I flinched, and Mom pulled me back a few feet. "Kaito, call the fire department." Her voice was urgent. "Max, stay here!"

The smoke curled around the starship like poisonous gas, and the stairs clanked to the metal floor. Mayor Zhang's facial expression rearranged into one of horror. Kaito tapped Mom's holopad, placing a localized order for help. Mom, however, surged forward, covering her mouth with the fabric of her shirt as a figure appeared at the top of the staircase.

A man.

I stared in shock as the newcomer staggered down the stairs, clutching a yellow mask to his nose and mouth. His pale skin was covered in soot, his sharp red hair muddled with it, and he missed the bottom step and almost crashed headlong into Mom.

Then, in the echoing silence of Hangar 42, he coughed into his arm, slumped to the ground, and said, hoarsely, "Whew. Don't try to fly one of these on your own. It is *not* a good idea."

And that's how I met Mr. Hames.

2

THE BIGGEST GALAXY IN THE SMALLEST CLASSROOM

The news of Mr. Hames's unorthodox arrival spread like wild-fire, and in the typical way of gossip on Azura, the stories warped far beyond reality. Pretty soon, he was a hit man, fleeing a mafia overlord by skirting the edges of the Fifth Star System. Or a pirate, suave and cunning, with illicit cargo stashed under the floorboards of his ship. Or a disgraced prince, escaping a rebellion on one of the inner terraformed planets.

This continued for three days, and in that glorious time, I ruled the classroom. Well, India and I did, because of course she got all the details when I slipped back into class. Together, we propped our feet on borrowed desks, wearing matching smirks as everyone attempted to bribe us for the truth.

Well, everyone except Mrs. Smith. An old crone who'd probably taught my grandparents, she would have retired years ago if Azura had the teachers to spare. The long-term babysitting had made her crotchety and bitter and *so* over our drama, especially after the smoke bomb. When she stomped into her classroom and saw the crowd surrounding us, she lifted her thin black cane and whapped her desk hard enough to turn heads.

"Enough gossip," she snarled, glaring at me with venom. "Get to your seats. Now!"

The kids scrambled away. Nashira, still holding a tray of meticulously decorated cupcakes her twin sister had baked, whispered, "Later?"

India flipped her long brown braid over her shoulder and cast me an appraising glance. But it was obvious we'd spill; Louisa's cupcakes were legendary, even if she was too shy to share them herself. But her sister, Nashira, had clearly brought out the big guns today. I nodded, and India plucked the frosted goodness from the tray. "Sure. After class, okay?"

"Sit down," Mrs. Smith growled again, and Nashira rejoined Louisa in the corner of the room.

India bent closer to me, flipping her feet off the desk when Mrs. Smith scowled at her. The moment the teacher turned away, she whispered, "Anything we tell Nashira will be public knowledge by noon."

Nashira valued communication—any form of communication. Especially gossip. Which meant she fit perfectly on Azura.

"I know," I replied. "We'll be stingy. But if we play this right, we can probably get a set of her comm-phones." Comm-phones were circular devices that hooked up to your ear, allowing instant, flawless communication even across the vacuum of space. India and I could wreak havoc all over Azura with a pair of those.

"Let's hope Echo isn't in her backpack today," she said. Microptera like Echo were tiny bat-like creatures bred to maintain the insect population in the botanarium. Except for Nashira's, which had somehow become a pet. A very strange, very gross pet. Couldn't blame India when she rolled her eyes and added, "Not sure I'd want the comm-phones then."

I snorted.

At the front of the room, Mrs. Smith smiled, wide and cold. Her usual class—Azura's thirteen-year-olds, who weren't nearly as annoyed with us younger kids as their teacher—shared looks of horror. It didn't take a mind reader to know what they'd realized: Mrs. Smith didn't smile. Ever.

I shuddered, sinking into my chair.

"Today is a good day," the old woman said, voice rasping and ominous. She tapped the cane against the white tile floor, scanning the intruders in her classroom. Seven of us, crammed against the outer edge of the room, desks pressed so close together we could barely squeeze between them. "Today, I get rid of you heathens."

Rhett smoothed his impeccable outfit; as heir to the biggest clothing shop on Azura, he always dressed like he was going to a Starmas Eve dinner. "You get rid of us until next year, you mean." He cast Tarynn Zhang a smirk. Usually, he reserved that tone for India and me, but apparently he was an equal-opportunity terrorizer today.

In the far corner, ignored by almost everyone, Arsenio laughed. When no one joined in, he hunched over his copy of *Surgical Simulator*. Some kids wanted normal VRs like *Starship Racer*, and some kids spent their days practicing surgery on a holographic image. Apparently.

Tarynn—ever the teacher's pet—glared at the boys, then politely raised her hand. "Does this mean we've found a substitute?"

I saw right through her disinterested tone. Mayor Zhang was too professional to gossip, and Tarynn was too proud to admit she cared, but I hadn't missed her sideways glances the last three days.

Now, she shot us a sly smile that spoke volumes. A new substitute was a big development . . . and depending on who they'd hired, it might even supersede our tight-lipped secrets about Mr. Hames.

Our relevance was slipping.

India took a bite of Louisa's cupcake, eyelids fluttering in bliss. "Good while it lasted," she whispered, the words garbled with rich chocolate cake.

I rolled my eyes.

"Yes, Ms. Zhang. That's exactly what that means," Mrs. Smith said curtly.

The room buzzed with this new information, louder than the honeybees in the botanarium. Mrs. Smith pounded the floor again with her cane. "Quiet. *Quiet!*" When silence reigned, she pointed at the door. "Once I introduce your new teacher, you will, in an *orderly fashion*, remove your desks from my class. I want calm and quiet as you return to your intended room. Is that clear?"

"Yes, ma'am," Tarynn chimed, folding her arms across her desk. Picture-perfect student.

Well. Couldn't have that. India and I smirked at each other, and she mouthed, "Smoke bomb?"

I snickered, but before I could flash a thumbs-up, our new substitute stepped into the room. Any thought of another disruption vanished. My jaw dropped.

The lanky, redheaded man offered a half-hearted wave.

"This is Mr. Hames," Mrs. Smith said.

The class *erupted*.

"Holy stars, it's the pirate—"

"He's not a pirate! Look at him. He's barely—"

"—can't believe it. Where do you think he's from—"

"—tourist! Teaching us? What the—"

"BE QUIET," Mrs. Smith roared, but it was too much. She dissolved into a coughing fit of bone-shattering hacks that rendered her speechless. Irately, she smacked her cane against the side of her desk. It didn't work.

Mr. Hames rubbed the back of his neck. "Ah, Natalia? W-would you like some water?"

"He's so *polite*." Rhett sniffed. It wasn't a compliment.

"Does this mean we don't have to take that exam on animal poaching next week?" Nashira asked hopefully, setting the platter of cupcakes on Louisa's desk. She twirled her leaf earrings; since their mother managed the botanarium where Echo was *supposed* to live, she always had new leaves pinned to her ears. She said it was a fashion statement. Rhett assured her it wasn't.

No one replied to her question, and she huffed in irritation.

Meanwhile, India shot a look of pure mischief in my direction. But for once, I couldn't return it. For once, I was knocked off-balance. I'd barely met Mr. Hames. The firefighters arrived almost immediately—not like they had far to go—and in the chaos, Mom had sent me back to class. It wasn't enough time to form a real opinion on him, despite my embellishments to my classmates.

But never in a million years had I imagined he'd take over our class.

Poor fool.

"Out," Mrs. Smith choked, and shoved her cane at the door. "Out of my room. All of you!"

Mr. Hames stood at her side, hesitating, which was weird. He must not have much experience in a classroom. Any other teacher would be taking control by this point.

Luckily for him, Tarynn flourished in this environment. She pushed to her feet and snapped her fingers. "You heard her. Get back to Room 7. Two people to a desk, and we'll take three trips. One for half the desks, one for the other half, one for the chairs. Move it!"

We'd been so cramped for space, none of us needed much encouragement, despite her barked orders. Mr. Hames held the door while we shuffled our desks back into the classroom down the corridor.

Room 7. Home of the twelve-year-olds of space station Azura.

"I missed this place," India remarked as we positioned her desk at her usual spot, beside the only porthole in the room. It overlooked the center cylinder of the wheel-like Azura, glowing gray amid a smattering of stars. Not much of a view, but better than a white wall.

"Yeah," I said distantly, my eyes trained on Mr. Hames as he dropped onto our old teacher's chair. He bounced twice, wrinkled his nose, and glanced at the massive holoscreen behind him. Maybe wherever he'd taught before had better equipment than we did, way out on Azura.

His obvious disdain made me scowl. For the first time, the dark word "intruder" passed through my mind. Tourists were usually a point of excitement, but he clearly wasn't pleased to be here. Like Azura was lesser, somehow, just because we were small and isolated. I bristled on behalf of my home.

"Hey." India poked my shoulder. "You're glaring. Something wrong?"

Mr. Hames looked right at me, recognition flashing in his eyes. He'd only met me for a second, and we'd barely exchanged names. If he thought he'd find a kindred spirit in me, he was mistaken.

I looked away. "No. Let's get my desk."

Ten minutes later, the twelfth-year class was back home, arranged in our usual fashion: desks spaced evenly in two rows, all facing the teacher. A teacher who didn't seem to know what to do with himself, now that he had the complete attention of seven kids.

He cleared his throat.

"Ah, hi. I'm Milo—er, Mr. Hames."

What kind of teacher introduced themselves by their first name?

Something about this guy wasn't adding up. Like the way he fumbled with the holoscreen—our outdated, edge-of-space equipment that any teacher should have known how to use. How he fidgeted under our stares, even though this was purely day one, introduction stuff. When he shuffled the lesson plan on his desk, squinting as if it were a totally different language.

"New guy's weird," India said under her breath.

So, she'd noticed it too.

"I heard that," Mr. Hames replied loudly. India stiffened, but he plowed ahead, exasperated now. "Look. I'm going to be honest. I don't want to be here. I bet none of you do either."

"I do." Tarynn pursed her lips.

Mr. Hames's eyes widened. "Seriously?" When she didn't object, he tossed up his hands. "What kind of kid are you?"

I pressed a fist against my lips to keep from snickering. India wasn't as kind. Her guffaws echoed through the room, and Tarynn spun toward her with a scowl.

In a rare moment, Louisa, our resident recluse, looked up from her customized holopad. Her thick glasses slipped down her nose, and she pushed them higher as she stuttered, "Sir . . . If you don't enjoy teaching, um . . . why are you here?"

Mr. Hames sighed. "What's your name?"

"Louisa," Nashira answered.

She did most of her sister's talking.

Mr. Hames ignored Nashira, though, focusing entirely on Louisa. "It's a pleasure. As it turns out, one person can't fly a starship built for eight. And when you try, it breaks." I stifled a snort. No kidding, genius. But Mr. Hames was already distracted, running his hands through his hair. "Even if you have places to be. Even if you only have three weeks to find—" He cut himself off, grinding his teeth. "But I digress. Point is, my ship broke, and I can't fix it without money."

Cheeks red, Louisa ducked back into her holopad. That response probably hadn't satisfied her, but one outspoken comment a year was more than we usually got.

India raised her hand. When Mr. Hames—naively—pointed at her, she said, "Hang on. Don't you own that starship? What happened to your crew?"

"Apparently, crews need to be paid," he replied, crossing his arms. "Weird, isn't it?"

"Very," she agreed good-naturedly, but a devious glint overtook her eyes. If Mr. Hames didn't watch his sarcasm, he'd be the recipient of a smoke bomb pretty soon. I grinned in anticipation.

But then Mr. Hames took a different turn. He stepped to the front of his desk, leaning against it. His tone was imploring. "Lemme ask you something. You kids ever been off this space station?"

Arsenio, arguably the most traveled among us—since his parents went to medical conferences at least once a year, and a few times they'd brought him too—hunched under our stares. "I mean, I've been to one or two of the Lucarro space stations. And we've *all* flown to the asteroid belt. It's, like, a rite of passage."

"The Lucarro space stations . . . and the asteroid belt," Mr. Hames repeated.

There it was again. That disdain. This time, I wasn't the only one bristling.

"Where else would we go?" Tarynn demanded.

"Where else—" Mr. Hames cut himself off, running his hands through his bright-red hair. "Oh stars, you kids. *Anywhere.* How about Surn, home of the last paloquoia tree? Its canopy takes up a quarter of the planet, with the most intricate root system you've ever seen! Or . . . or Spichi. It's got an ocean with enough oxygen you can still breathe—think *literal* mermaids. Or maybe Baelia—a literal mesh of every culture in every star system. Immigrants from every colonized planet, with enough food and music and museums to keep you busy for three lifetimes."

He got more excited as he talked, pacing the front of the classroom, waving his hands as if he could enthuse us into understanding. And it kind of worked. I found myself leaning forward, thinking of swimming for hours without surfacing for breath, or immersing myself in thousands of cultures at once.

I mean, gotta admit, that'd be airtight.

But it didn't change the fact that no one on Azura traveled that far, had seen that much. It just wasn't how life worked. So, when Mr. Hames swept us with a desperate, questioning stare, all he got was silence.

He seemed to deflate, hunching into himself. "Aww, kids. That's not even counting what you can find in the vacuum of space." His words were mumbled, disappointed.

Tarynn hated disappointing teachers. She straightened and said, "Trick statement. There's nothing in the vacuum of space."

"Nothing in space?" Mr. Hames exclaimed.

A memory slammed into me, stealing my breath. Of Mom and me eating at the kitchen table, of Dad strolling in after a site visit to whatever asteroid had been mined that day. Of him laughing and sweeping Mom into a hug and whispering, *"I saw it again."*

Mom pressed a hand against his chest, rolling her eyes, deadpanning, *"Just floating in space, hmm?"*

"Not floating, Camille. Swimming!"

She'd laughed. I'd asked what he was talking about, but Dad just winked at me.

Two weeks later, The Accident happened, and he was gone.

I gripped my desk, and for the first time, curiosity overrode the dull grief of old memories. I'd forgotten about that conversation. What had Dad seen, way out in the asteroid belt?

"Nothing in space," Mr. Hames repeated with a hollow chuckle. He shook his head at Tarynn. "You have *no* idea."

"What?" Tarynn gaped.

Shaking his head, Mr. Hames circled his desk and sank into the chair. "Whatever. Let's get this over with. Access your . . . um . . . whatever you were working on with the last teacher."

We glanced at each other. Tarynn looked horrified, but Arsenio said, "I mean, I guess we were reading about animal poaching." And he pushed his VR game aside to tap the school-issued holopad on his desk. We slowly followed suit.

In the rummaging of students, Mr. Hames plucked Mr. Bruska's vintage handheld calendar off the desk, squinting at it. When he thought we weren't listening, he muttered, "Three weeks. I've got to get off this station."

3

THE MUSIC OF COMMUNICATION

"Well, *he* has no idea what he's doing," India remarked after class, once we'd put distance between Room 7 and the strange Mr. Hames.

I pressed my lips together. "It's weird, isn't it? Like, why bother accepting this job? Azura's shorthanded in a lot of areas."

"Maybe Tarynn's mom begged him," she joked, slipping her hands into one of the many pockets of her patchwork jacket. It was always kind of cold on Azura. No matter how realistic the faux-wood floors seemed, or what cheery color Mayor Zhang chose to paint the curved bulkhead walls every few years, it didn't change the fact that space stations were sculpted with metal.

"A Zhang? *Begging*?" With a scoff, I moved closer to her, letting a few older kids pass at a run. They laughed and shoved each other, then jammed the button to call an elevator. A soft ding and they were gone, and the hall went quiet again.

India shrugged. "Well, think about it. An entire class teacherless for upward of three weeks? And her daughter's class, no less? I bet the other parents are getting on her case for that."

"Maybe."

"It's my favorite theory." She grinned, pressing the button to call our own elevator. I busied myself by playing with the gravity, or lack thereof. A single leap near the elevators could propel you almost into the ceiling.

My stomach twisted as weightlessness captured me, just for a few moments. But India wasn't paying attention. Although her short, dark hair floated like a halo around her face, she kept her feet on the ground, gripping the support handle on the wall. Weird.

When the elevator dinged open, we stepped inside. But she just squinted at the panel of buttons, one for each level of Azura. "Same fifteen floors. Same fifteen destinations."

"I mean, if there was suddenly a sixteenth floor, I'd be pretty freaked out."

She rolled her eyes at me but went silent.

I poked her shoulder. "Why? What's wrong?"

"It's nothing."

"Oh, okay." I shoved off the floor, using the funky gravity to bounce over her, stabbing the button for the recreation level. As the lift began to move, I steadied myself against the back wall and waited.

India didn't handle silence well.

I counted:

Three.

Two.

One.

She cracked, her words spilling out in a rush. "It's just—a planet of mermaids? A tree that takes up a quarter of a planet?

Maybe . . . I don't know. If that's what's out there, maybe my dad really did 'go traveling.'"

My smirk vanished. India and I didn't talk about our fathers. The few times we'd tried, one or both of us wound up in tears, which was, like, the *least* fun you could have on Azura. But there was always this unspoken thread between us, this knowledge that although we were both dad-less, our experiences were very different.

Because at least I knew, without a doubt, what had happened to my dad. At least he hadn't wanted to leave Mom and me.

India plucked at an unraveled string on her jacket, then paused when her fingers brushed one of the dozens of metal travel patches her father had collected . . . before. Each one depicted a different destination in the Fifth Star System, laser-engraved emblems bearing their flag or unique feature. "They're kitschy things," her mother had said the day India decided to sew them onto the jacket, "picked up in any station gift shop. He didn't spend any real effort on that, sweetie."

But to India, they were as valuable as anemonium was to Azurans.

Her voice was barely a whisper, colored with the tiniest ray of hope. "I mean, if Dad really is just traveling, maybe one day he'll come back."

Oh stars. I swallowed, my mouth suddenly dry. Some dark, selfish part of me didn't want to think about her dad coming back—not when mine never could.

And worse, I didn't want India hoping, only to realize that Mr. Hames was right, that some people didn't want to stay on

Azura. Some people counted down the days until they could escape and never, ever return.

Which was worse? Living with false hope or drowning in real grief?

I didn't want to know the answer.

The lift dinged, double doors opening into a long hallway. This one was painted a leafy green, with private tables and comfy chairs leading to a bustling common space. The recreation floor was larger than the education level, crammed with ball courts and a community garden and a crafting center and even a little coffee shop run by Ms. Jakubowski.

It was packed. The workday wasn't over—considering most people did shift work, it rarely was—but school was out for the day, and on a space station this small, there weren't many other places for us to go.

I loved it. We never had to travel far to find something interesting, or someone to hang out with. But India scanned the open area, and for the first time, dissatisfaction flashed across her features.

A cold lump settled in my stomach, this terribly certain knowledge that something had changed.

And it was Mr. Hames's fault.

"Come on," I said, taking her hand. "I've got a song for you."

India smiled, a little forced, but allowed herself to be tugged through the crowd. "Aren't you meeting Mr. Keller today?"

"In an hour. Plenty of time."

We weaved through the garden. At the coffee shop, Ms. Jakubowski poured a cup of tea with homegrown leaves while

Suki, one of the teenagers, kicked her girlfriend's butt in basketball at a court nearby. A little blond girl sprinted in front of us, followed by one of Mom's friends, Maria. She shot us an apologetic look. "Sorry, Max. India." Then she raised her voice: "Rose, don't you dare make me say it again!"

The little girl screeched and ducked behind a planter of lilacs.

I grinned. This place was *home*. Why would anyone want to leave?

"Someone's in trouble," I whispered as Maria crept around the planter, huffing exasperation. A few seconds later, Rose squealed and Maria laughed.

"Hmm?" India pulled her gaze from the bank of windows, from the glimmering stars beyond the clear plastiglass. "Oh. I guess so."

My jaw set. Music. Music fixed everything. With a newfound desperation, I towed India along until we reached the back corner of the recreation level. There weren't really corners on a cylindrical space station, but someone had built a closet to house old equipment, stuff waiting to be repurposed. With the humidity of the garden, the lock had rusted away years ago.

Now, I eased it open, making sure no one saw. When the coast was clear, India slipped past me, settling onto her gnarled mess of netting. She always looked like a queen, perched on a knotted throne. It made me feel like her bard, and with a flourish, I plucked Dad's prized decivox from its hiding spot.

At a glance, it didn't look broken. Cracks spidered along the wood's varnish, but overall the instrument was intact. Even though it was shaped like a tiny guitar, the decivox was closer to a theremin. There were no strings. Instead, two metal rods—one secured to the neck, one at the base—acted as capacitors, reacting to movement in its electric field. Three knobs on the grip controlled volume, and twirling my fingers crafted the music.

My fingers brushed the metal rods; I winced as they wobbled under my touch. They'd come loose somehow, and reattaching them properly required tools I couldn't hope to find on Azura. The sound was always kind of . . . off. Higher-pitched, screechier. It was still fun to play, but no one would be requesting concerts anytime soon.

Not until I could afford to send it to the inner planets for a real tuning. I even had a shop picked out: Skee's Music Emporium, "best instrument repair in the Fifth Star System." Just a few more months, and I'd be able to play for Mom, to show her my true talent.

And then she'd understand I wasn't only good at engineering.

Lucky for me, India never cared about poor tuning. She grinned as I dropped to the floor, lowering my fingers to the hole between the metal rods.

"And now, from the vast corners of space," I said in the deepest tone I could muster, which of course meant my voice squeaked embarrassingly instead. My cheeks colored as India giggled, but at least she was laughing now. I played up the drama. "A sound, a *musician*, found only on a tiny space station in the middle of nowhere. I present Maxion Belmont and his decivox!"

"Whoo!" India clapped.

Happiness swept through me at her enthusiasm. Though, to be fair, I was rarely *unhappy* playing the decivox. Ever since I'd found it in my parents' closet, I was obsessed. But when Mom saw me fiddling with it, she'd burst into tears; apparently, the decivox used to be Dad's favorite instrument too.

I wished I could have heard him play.

I started soft and slow, wiggling my thumb and forefinger in a slight vibrato. The instrument screeched, making me wince, but I'd had over a year of practice with the poor tuning. I adjusted appropriately, using my pinky to hold down one of the rickety metal rods as the rest of my hand coaxed a song from the hollow belly. My fingers fiddled with the dials near my other hand, starting the music mellow and quiet.

It was like storytelling, the grandest form of communication. I'd heard the vids. A truly skilled musician could weave a narrative of sound into something gorgeous, impacting. They could tell a tale with notes and beats.

Today was not one of those days for me.

India closed her eyes, even as the instrument screeched again. Gritting my teeth, I forced my way through the grating sounds to find the softer melody. I played until the lines between her eyebrows smoothed, until the downward tilt of her lips evened out, until her cheeks lifted in a smile. And then, only then, did I crank the dials, ending the song with a sharp yank of my hand.

India clapped again, but this time it was earnest, awestruck.

"Okay, Max. Come on. That was incredible!"

I blushed. I mean, she was my friend; she had to say that. But the euphoria of hearing it out loud was always overwhelming. "Maybe once it gets fixed, it will be."

India shoved my shoulder. "You're great now, you weirdo.

Why are you waiting to play for your mom again? If you showed her what you can do, I bet she'd pay to get it fixed right now!"

"The last time I played for her, she cried." I gestured at the cluttered storage closet. "Why do you think I play here?"

But we'd had this discussion before, and India wasn't listening. Her eyes grew wide, her grin bigger than the Kialoa Nebula. "Oooh. What if you played for her, and she was so touched and amazed she sent you off for professional study at the inner planets? Stars, Max, you could be the person that puts Azura back on the map!"

The happiness of making music curdled like sour milk. "I don't want Azura back on the map," I said stubbornly. "I like how it is right now."

India rolled her eyes. "What? A dying space station the universe forgot?"

"No. Our home." I didn't bother keeping the hurt from my voice.

The silence between us grew awkward. I stowed my decivox in its meticulous hiding place so I wouldn't have to meet her gaze anymore.

India fidgeted, then cleared her throat. "I'm just saying, it'd be cool if we got more tourists than *Mr. Hames*. Maybe the next ones won't be so weird." Then she nudged me, offering a wink.

Trying to get things back to normal.

Well, better than fighting. I laughed, even though I didn't feel it. "I think if we had another set of tourists, Mayor Zhang would freak. And then Tarynn would be even more high-strung than she is now."

"You're right." She mock-shuddered. "Best to keep Azura a secret."

But I don't think she believed it.

4

THE OUTSTANDING TALENT OF CLASSROOM 7

The next morning, I came to class with a bit of baggage.

Specifically, a hertz-rated infibrillator for a Hammock G56 mineship. If that sounded fancy, good. Keep believing that. Because it was certainly better than the reality: that Mr. Keller sent me home with an overly complicated thermometer and orders to have it repaired by the end of the week.

Considering the fact that I used to work side by side with Dad on *real* starship parts—slipstream generators and mining claws and the like—this was a bit patronizing. But Mr. Keller was the one paying, so I did as asked.

The infibrillator thunked onto my desk, leaving grease smears on the plastic surface. I sank into my chair and glanced at the clock. Thirty minutes before class started, and no one was here. I savored the quiet moment, diving into my work.

Right until Arsenio, the freckled would-be doctor of our class, arrived. His bright eyes centered on me, utterly oblivious of how I hunched to make myself smaller. A smile spread across his lips, and he strolled over.

I swallowed a groan as he dropped into India's empty seat.

"Hey, Max. What'cha working on?"

"Infibrillator," I said, pointedly staring at the piece of machinery. It looked kind of like a toaster, but with more moving parts than an old-timey watch. I cracked the seals on the side, then plucked my hydrodriver from my pocket.

Maybe if I didn't look at Arsenio, he'd go away.

But he wasn't great at recognizing social cues. It took about two minutes of tilting his head this way and that before he interrupted again. "That looks messier than heartworm. I mean, minus the blood. And the wiggly wigglies." He cracked a grin, waggling his fingers as if they were the parasite in question.

That was the thing about Arsenio. His dad was the station veterinarian, and his mom was one of our surgeons. So he'd been moving between operating rooms since he was little. A normal conversation in his household was *not* normal elsewhere.

Don't get me wrong. I'm all for gross conversations. Up until two years ago, Arsenio and I actually used to be really good friends. But Arsenio wasn't great at talking about anything else, and after The Accident, I didn't really want to know how skin blistered after third-degree burns.

I grunted acknowledgment, powering the thin hydrodriver with the flick of my finger. The mechanisms whirred to life, offering me a compact tool that could do nearly anything with the right attachment. It took just a few seconds to switch the screwdriver piece out for a flathead that measured torque. Then I delved into my project.

Arsenio hovered for about ten minutes, despite the awkward

silence. That's when India threw open the classroom door, scanned the room, and said, "Replacing me already, Max?"

Things had been weird between us since last night, so I was eager to get back to normal. Maybe that was why I replied, curtly, "Not by choice."

It was supposed to be a joke, but it came out mean. Arsenio's expression crumbled, his face paling with embarrassment. It made his freckles stand out like tiny suns. My stomach churned with guilt, so I grinned his way, attempting damage control.

Too late. His shoulders hunched, and he sulked back to his own desk, positioned at the opposite corner of the room.

India watched him leave, then frowned. "Lemme guess. Blood and guts?"

"Heartworm today," I mumbled.

Across the room, Arsenio blinked hard, then pulled out the flat disc and powered up *Surgical Simulator*. The golden image twisted under his hands as he chose a surgery and delved into its process.

A part of me wanted to apologize, but it was hard to be casual around the kid whose mom had operated on my dad.

Hard to be friends with the family who couldn't save him.

The rest of the class trickled in. The twins arrived, with Nashira chatting amicably while Louisa listened. India nudged me, and we both fell silent, straining to hear Nashira's fast-whispered gossip: "—can't believe you didn't know. Uncle Amir had to arrest—" Then she realized we were listening and interrupted herself: "Hey, Belmont, Kitlowski. If you wanna know, you better have something to trade for it." She dissolved into laughter. Louisa shot us a sympathetic smile, adjusting the grip on her holopad.

"Ouch," India said. "I mean, that was deserved, but still. Ouch." When they turned around, India stuck out her tongue at them.

I snorted.

They took their seats next to Arsenio. Louisa smiled at him, but Nashira kept talking, and Louisa clearly couldn't decide who deserved her attention. She settled on her sister, offering a sympathetic look before redirecting herself toward Nashira's monologue.

Arsenio sighed and looked back at his game. My heart twisted in guilt yet again.

I shouldn't have said what I did; it was mean. But honestly, at this point, I didn't know *what* to say to Arsenio. And so, quietly discontent, I let India fill the silence as I tinkered with my project.

Tarynn and Rhett strolled into the room last, exactly five minutes before class was scheduled to start. Tarynn was talking pointedly about a fancy dinner Mayor Zhang was hosting—which of course Rhett's parents were invited to.

Rhett smirked and said, too loudly, "We wouldn't miss your mother's delightful steak dinners."

I scowled. Subtle. He knew most of us couldn't afford that kind of meat. But Rhett was already moving on, running his fingers along the fabric of Tarynn's sleeve. "And I'll have Father sew you something new. Maybe with lace? You loved that last time."

Tarynn grinned. "Well, who doesn't love lace?"

"I could name a few," Rhett replied, and shot a disdainful

look at India's outfit, the same patchwork jacket with the travel badges, handcrafted (and not well), with ripped pants and clunky boots. In short, it was chaotic and wonderful, just like India, but Rhett still sniffed disdainfully. "But I suppose even that atrocity is better than Max, clutching that hydrodriver like a security blanket. Here I thought we weren't kids anymore."

They burst into snobbish laughter, taking their seats.

I bristled and whispered under my breath, "How do you think he'd react if I smeared grease all over that tailored vest?" I rubbed the grit between my blackened fingers.

India chuckled. "Oh stars. I'll be peeling you off the bulkhead."

Might be worth it. But India struck up another conversation, and I settled for glaring at the back of Rhett's head instead. This was always how life went on Azura. Everyone knew everyone, but we'd all paired off a few years ago into cliques. Once, we'd have formed a circle and chatted as real friends, but these days . . .

Well, these days, not many people understood India and me. At least we had each other. We chatted aimlessly while the clock ticked forward, keeping Standard Galactic Time.

7:59 a.m.

8:00 a.m.

8:05 a.m.

"Where is Mr. Hames?" Tarynn demanded.

"Maybe we scared him off," India suggested.

Tarynn whipped around. "What did you do?"

She put a hand over her heart, feigning mortal offense. "It wasn't me! If I'd done it, you'd know. I'm not subtle."

I laughed and delved back into the infibrillator. It didn't take long to figure out the problem: a tiny plastic fan had broken during operation, jamming the inner mechanisms. If I could unclog the gears and replace the fan, the machine should function okay.

My hydrodriver hummed as I poked and prodded. Tarynn shifted her glare to me, then began pacing the front of the classroom. The rest of us kept ourselves entertained for a while, but when the clock struck 8:20 a.m., almost everyone had fallen silent to watch Tarynn muttering under her breath. She hated tardiness.

Her ire was kind of amusing when you weren't on the receiving end.

Of course, the moment she tossed her hands upward and stomped toward the door, it swung open to reveal Mr. Hames, disheveled and annoyed. His stormy expression silenced Tarynn's tirade before she could even begin.

Quietly, she slid into her seat, but her irritated scowl never left. Ten digits said the mayor would be hearing about this at that fancy steak dinner.

Mr. Hames stomped to his desk, pulling at his messy red hair. "You know what's terrible? School. Who in their right mind would be in this tiny box of a room when there's a galaxy to explore?"

His white shirt was streaked with black, ripped over the left shoulder. With little regard for his clothes, Mr. Hames scrubbed grease-stained hands on his pants. Rhett stifled a gasp, clearly appalled.

On the other hand, I was mildly impressed. According to Mr. Keller's shop gossip last night, Mr. Hames knew next to nothing about the inner workings of his own ship. But that clearly didn't stop him from trying to get it spaceborne again.

Which was . . . kind of stupid, if you didn't know what you were doing.

Mr. Hames growled, still ranting. "I mean, sure. Exploring is all well and good. But to do it, you need a ship. Which, of course, I have. Except I don't. You kids ever try to repair a broken slipstream generator?"

It sounded rhetorical, but the rest of the class swiveled to face me. Under their pointed stares, I shrugged. "Well, yeah. A few times."

"Because it's stars-darned aw—" Mr. Hames cut himself off, eyebrows shooting almost to his hair. "Wait. Max. What did you say?"

Huh. He remembered my name. I repeated, slowly, "A few times. Azura's main export is anemonium. You know, the stuff they use to purify air supplies on every space station and ship in the galaxy? Can't mine that if we don't have working spacecraft." As if he were stupid, I gestured at the hertz-rated infibrillator on my desk.

His eyes dropped to the piece of machinery, and he inhaled sharply. "Are you any good?"

"His dad was the lead engineer," Nashira replied. Then her face colored, and she mumbled, "You know . . . ah, before." She whispered the last part so quietly I doubt Mr. Hames heard. Then she shot me an awkward, apologetic look.

I glared back. At my side, India whispered, "Subtle."

She was the only one here who really understood me lately.

I tried to ignore the dark, sick feeling in my chest as Mr. Hames blinked.

"Your dad—?"

"He's dead," I muttered. "Don't get excited."

"Oh, jeez, Max. Sorry to hear that." Mr. Hames rubbed his jaw, smearing grease over his chin. "But back up a few paces. You can really fix starships? That's incredible! You're what? Ten?"

Was that supposed to be a compliment? Irritation colored my voice. "We're all twelve." And you'd think the substitute teacher of Azura's *twelfth-year class* would know that.

Before Mr. Hames could reply, Tarynn sniffed. "Max isn't special. All of our parents or relatives teach us their practical skills. We're the future of Azura, you know." Now her eyes narrowed, and her voice became vaguely threatening. "Which is great, but it won't mean anything if we don't get a solid foundation *in the classroom*." Although I couldn't see her face, Tarynn's glare wasn't difficult to imagine.

And still, Mr. Hames barely acknowledged her. He scanned the rest of the class, focusing on every single kid. His eyes darted to the holopad in Louisa's hands. The comm-phone poking out of Nashira's backpack. The medical game Arsenio was fiddling with.

And suddenly, his grin spread, brighter than a supernova.

"Wait. There are seven of you!"

"So?" India drummed her fingers on her desk.

"Max. What's the crew complement of a Tracker Mark VI?"

"Eight," I replied suspiciously.

Mr. Hames laughed, slapping his knee. "Yes! Grab your bags, kiddos. We're going on a field trip!"

5

AN EYE FOR ADVENTURE

"I think he's kidnapping us," India whispered, more amused than scared. "That's gotta be what's happening, right? Like, he's going to coax us onto his ship and fly away, and no one will ever know."

We stood at the back of the class. A few feet ahead, Mr. Hames keyed in a code to access Hangar 42, where his starship, the *Calypso*, was still docked.

I shoved my hands into my pockets. "Well, my mom would know. Just opening this door sends a ping to her office." I smirked, imagining the storm she'd bring when she discovered Mr. Hames, our substitute teacher, outside his classroom during school hours.

And all of us with him.

I mean, points for keeping us supervised, I guess.

The doors slid open, and Mr. Hames jogged into the massive docking bay. When none of us moved to follow, he huffed and spun back around. "Come on, come on! No time to waste."

"India thinks you're going to kidnap us," I said, jerking a thumb at her. She elbowed me, and we both started laughing.

Mr. Hames blinked. "What? Oh, stars, no. We're not leaving the airlock." His words held weight, like he forgot to tack on "*today*." Before I could comment on it, he moved right along.

"I told you, it's just a field trip." Then he frowned and added, "Those are a thing, right?"

India and I shared a wry glance. Sure. He was a real teacher. Just like India was a dodabia tamer, or I was a ballet dancer.

Nashira frowned. "I mean, two years ago we visited the waste processing plant on level 1. Our aunt worked there—but it was pretty gross."

"Hey, that reminds me. Isn't your *uncle* chief of police?" India asked, quirking a grin when Mr. Hames paled a bit. Louisa frowned, but I flashed India a thumbs-up. Way to make the new guy sweat.

Mr. Hames tugged at his collar. "Wait. Wait. Listen. My starship is broken, and I—I just need some help. The mechanics here want to charge me a month's pay to fix it. But I *have* to be off this space station sooner than that."

As someone who'd spent a whole year saving every digit for something far less expensive, that annoyed me. I crossed my arms. "What's the rush?"

"Obviously, he owes someone money," Rhett drawled.

Arsenio cleared his throat, tucking his surgery game disc into his pocket. "Hang on. I thought he was a prince, fleeing his—"

"Stars! Is gossiping all you people do?" Mr. Hames asked.

There it was again. That disdain for Azura and the people on it. How dare he judge us? This—this *outsider*. I couldn't keep the irritation from my voice. "Then clear it up for us. What are you doing here? Who are you?"

The silence was tangible. Mr. Hames rubbed the back of his neck. "I'm an explorer."

"That's not a job," I said. "Try again."

"No, it's true! All I've done is travel, all my life. Max, come on. You've seen my starship. And your mom said you recognized the exhaust from my Starkwil generator. You think I'd invest in that if I didn't take exploration seriously?"

My classmates stared at me, but for once, I didn't have a reply. Because he was right. A Starkwil generator cost more than an engineer on Azura made in a decade. No idea how he got the money for one, but it must have taken him ages to save for it.

Yet, despite his earnest expression, my gut still whispered *lies*.

Mr. Hames gestured at his ship again, helplessly. "Do you know how hard it is to be an explorer with a broken ship? It's like—like trying to make a call without comm-phones."

Nashira stiffened, expression mortified.

"Or . . . I don't know"—Mr. Hames's eyes dropped to Arsenio—"a doctor without a patient." Then he glanced at Louisa. "A techie without a holopad."

Or a musician without an instrument.

Huh. So that's why he spoke with such passion. Like me, raving about my decivox. Suddenly, Mr. Hames's desperation made sense. The starship, the *Calypso*, was his broken instrument.

India must have been thinking the same thing, because she shot me a knowing glance. When I averted my gaze, she nudged me.

Fine, *fine*.

I stepped forward. "Assuming we help you, what's in it for us?"

Mr. Hames grinned, exuberant, but Tarynn cut him off, her

voice cross. "Hang on. We can't just spend our class time here, fixing your ship. We're supposed to be *learning*. That's why we're in school."

Mr. Hames thought for a moment. "Okay. Go with me here. You kids are all about hands-on experience, right? Your relatives teach you what they know, and then you go out and do it. The next generation."

"Yeah." Tarynn set her jaw. "So?"

"So"—Mr. Hames grinned—"what's more hands-on than fixing a real, actual starship? Learning to operate as a team, instead of ignoring each other in a classroom?" He held out his hands, backtracking. "Wait, sorry. Not a team. A *crew*."

The other kids murmured about how that might actually be airtight. Arsenio, especially, bounced on his heels. But when his eyes met mine, his expression faltered, and his brows knitted in question. As if he was *asking* me for permission.

To be fair, I didn't really want to be crew members with him. But that shouldn't change *his* mind, for stars' sake. Guilt curdled in my stomach again, and I forced a pained smile. Damage control, even if it was a pathetic attempt.

Arsenio beamed in response, as if I'd give him the sun instead of pinched lips.

Oblivious to our silent conversation, Nashira moved the discussion forward: "So, we'd each get jobs? Our parents won't let us touch anything on their ship. Especially not the radios." She clutched her backpack straps, snorting. "As if I don't know proper communication is vital."

Louisa laughed softly, elbowing her sister in a rare display of affection. "Maybe if you stopped taking Echo from the botanarium. Mom said they only have fifteen microptera to handle the insec—"

"Microptera?" Mr. Hames interrupted, perplexed.

Louisa clamped her mouth shut.

Nashira, on the other hand, swelled. "Well, I don't have him now—Arsenio's dad is doing checkups on the creatures in the botanarium today."

Well, that was risky, putting Echo's life in the hands of Arsenio's parents.

. . . Okay, that was mean. I was suddenly glad I hadn't spoken it out loud, especially after just trying to smooth things over with Arsenio. But the grim memory of The Accident was a black cloud in my mind, and it seemed to justify the words. Defiantly, I let them sit on the tip of my tongue, although I kept my mouth shut.

Nashira kept chatting about Echo. "I'll show him to you sometime, Mr. Hames! Microptera are like fancy bats. Best communicators on the space station . . . besides me, of course."

Tarynn and Rhett exchanged judgmental looks.

Mr. Hames cleared his throat. "Well, I've never been great with the communication equipment. Sounds like you're a perfect fit."

Nashira squeaked excitement, literally bouncing on her toes.

"What do you think, Louisa?" Mr. Hames asked, regaining the mousy girl's attention. She lowered her holopad, shifting uncomfortably, right until Mr. Hames said, "The *Calypso* has a pretty great computer. Might need some calibration after my little mishap."

Her eyes lit up. Well, that hadn't taken much persuasion.

"Ah, do you think anyone might get hurt?" Arsenio asked.

"Oh, no. It's perfectly safe—" Mr. Hames started, but then noticed his crestfallen expression. Our teacher tugged his collar again. "Although it's always good to have someone on first aid, just in case."

Arsenio's fingers ghosted over his surgical game. "Really?"

I narrowed my eyes at him. Seriously, who hoped for people to get hurt? Why couldn't he just be normal like the rest of us?

But before I could voice that, Rhett stepped forward, catching Mr. Hames's gaze. He barely spared a glance at Tarynn, who was irritated and showing it, as he said, "Sounds like a crew also needs a uniform."

"That they do," Mr. Hames agreed, a slow smile quirking his lips.

Rhett smirked back, smoothing his impeccable vest. "You're new here, but my family handles all the clothing needs of Azura." Well, that was a bald-faced lie. They had competition. Although even *I* couldn't deny I'd choose the Resnik wares over crotchety Mrs. Loans's old-man clothes any day.

Mr. Hames rubbed his chin. "What's your name?"

"Rhett."

"Sounds like you're offering, Rhett."

And the haughty bully of our class tilted his head and replied, coolly, "Guess I am."

Mr. Hames held out his fist, and Rhett bumped it.

Behind him, Tarynn gasped indignantly. Her face was getting redder and redder, which was pretty funny, not gonna lie. I tried to shoot India a dry glance—*Can you believe this?*—but she was totally ignoring me. In fact, she'd thrown her shoulders back like she was next in line.

"Come on," I whispered. "You aren't really buying this."

India grinned. "What's the alternative? Boring class?"

Oh. Well, she had a point. I heaved a fake long-suffering sigh to hide my smile. This was insane, but honestly? I was aching to dive into that Starkwil generator.

Dad would have been so jealous.

I stilled, realizing something. For the first time, I wasn't sad thinking about him. I imagined telling him about this, watching him groan and pout about the unfairness of it all, complaining that *I* got to fix it, not him . . . but the second he thought I wasn't listening, he'd have whispered to Mom, "*That's my boy.*"

My breath caught with the certainty of it. Stars darn it all, I wanted to make him proud.

Even if he wasn't here to see it.

"I'm in," I said.

"Me too!" India exclaimed.

And then Tarynn had to go and ruin it all. She crossed her arms, donned her signature scowl. "Hang on. *I* was elected class president, and I say we can't have class in a starship. Either we go back to Classroom 7, or I'm telling my mother." When Mr. Hames squinted, Tarynn grumbled in exasperation. "You know. The *mayor*?"

For a moment, it had really felt like we'd banded together in a way we hadn't in years, and then Tarynn just . . . ripped it away. We all glowered at her. Everyone except Rhett, who shifted uncomfortably, clearly torn between his controlling friendship with Tarynn and his newfound desire to design outfits for an entire crew. But this was a group effort, and we all knew it. If even one person snitched, it'd be over.

Especially if someone snitched to Mayor Zhang.

Yet instead of begging or pleading, Mr. Hames thought for a moment. "So Azura's a democracy, is what you're saying."

". . . Yes," Tarynn replied, as if it might be a trick question.

"Well, on a starship, the captain is the final authority. That's me, on the *Calypso*. But I usually have a first officer. They act kind of like a vice president, ready to take command if the captain is incapacitated. They also handle the day-to-day crew dynamics, settling arguments and things. Because of your experience as class president, I was going to offer it to you . . . but if you'd rather have an election . . ."

India and I burst out laughing. Sneaky, making Tarynn participate in another election when it could have been handed to her. Of course, Mr. Hames didn't understand how Tarynn operated—she may be bossy and rude, but she was also *excellent* at controlling a classroom—and campaigning. The chocolate bars she handed out before her speech definitely hadn't hurt her chances.

But now that he'd opened it up to the rest of us, the seeds of chaos had been planted. With a grin, India—who I knew for a fact didn't even want the position—stepped forward, chest swelling. She'd be a disaster in management, but I definitely wanted to see this. I began chanting, "India for officer. India for officer. India for officer!"

Tarynn shot us a nasty stare, but before she could reply, the *click-click-click* of heels echoed down the corridor.

Everyone froze.

Oh, right. I'd forgotten about Mom.

"Mr. Hames," she called when she was close enough. "Is there a problem?"

"Ah, hello, Camille." Our substitute teacher blinked, wide and innocent. "Why—ah, why would there be a problem?"

"Maybe because, without approval, you're taking my son's entire class into a hangar with just one airlock between them and the vacuum of space? I must admit, Milo, that's a very thin margin of error."

Oooh, she sounded mad. I hunched against her ire, even though, for once, it wasn't directed at me. Mr. Hames laughed nervously. They were probably the same age, and he towered over her, but we all knew who held the power here.

"Actually, I am trained on operating airlocks—"

Mom's eyes flashed. "Interesting. You said you were a teacher. Which is it, Milo?"

He blinked. "Can't I have more than one interest?"

A few of the kids snickered, and Mom's eyes coasted over us. Lips pinched, she motioned for Mr. Hames to follow her a few steps away—undoubtedly to avoid the gossip. It was a wise move.

But even her hushed whispers couldn't be muffled in the empty expanse of the hallway. Especially since the class had fallen eerily silent to eavesdrop.

Mom didn't notice. She turned her back to us, but her voice was curt. "I know the mayor approved you, but this does not look good, Milo. You've had control of the class for less than two days, and you're already deviating from their curriculum. What were you hoping to accomplish?"

But before Mr. Hames could attempt a reply, Tarynn stepped forward. Apparently, her desire to be first officer also made her *invincible*, based on how she intercepted my mother's dark gaze. Her voice was steady, matter-of-fact:

"Ms. Belmont, this is imperative to our education. Mr. Hames was showing us his starship. It's a Tracker Mark VI, you know. Even has a Starkwil generator. Max tells me those are rare."

Stars, she was good.

Not that I expected anything less. Tarynn was such a perfect student that adults inherently trusted her to be mature and honest. Mom scrutinized her expression, but Tarynn was a lot better at lying than I was. After a moment, Mom said, doubtfully, "Oh. Well . . . I mean, that's not really in your curriculum, is it?"

"It's a field study program we were planning," Tarynn replied, self-assuredly. "Ideally, it'll be a week long, where we learn the physics of slipstream generators through practical application. We'll be asking my mom tonight for formal permission."

India's jaw dropped. I elbowed her, and she quickly rearranged her face into boredom, which was exactly how she'd look if we really *were* learning the physics of slipstream generators.

But that *was* impressive. Not only had Tarynn found an excuse for today, but she'd also built in a reason for us to be out of the classroom for at least a week. Even Mr. Hames's eyebrows quirked upward at her words.

But we weren't out of the nebula yet. Mom turned to me next, a question in her eyes.

Keep it cool, Belmont. Face smooth, tone even. Just another day at class. I shrugged, even as sweat trickled down the back of my neck. "You're the one who keeps reminding me that hands-on experience builds character."

She squinted. For a moment, I couldn't breathe. She'd figured it out. I was so busted.

But then she said, "I suppose that's true. This is a rare opportunity."

What was *happening*?

Mr. Hames beamed. "I promise the students are perfectly safe with me, Camille. If you'd like to accompany us, you're more than welcome—"

"No, thank you." Mom pulled a holopad from her pocket, expanding it with a flick. "The weekly shipment from the inner planets is being unloaded in Hangar 13, I'm afraid they need me there."

"Ah," Mr. Hames said, and darn it all if he didn't sound disappointed. "Well, if you change your mind, you know where to find us. And in case you were wondering, I worked in a cargo bay very similar to this one while I put myself through school. I promise I'm familiar with airlock safety protocols."

Mom blushed. "Ah, of course. I'm sorry for assuming." Her eyes dropped to mine, and her tone firmed a bit. "Max. Listen to your teacher. No funny business. You too, India."

"I'll keep them in line," Tarynn promised. We would have

retorted, but I was too busy being utterly flabbergasted at how this had played out.

Mom chuckled. "I know you will, honey. Have fun, kids. Learn a lot, and be safe." With a wave, she strolled down the corridor, toward Hangar 13

The moment she was out of sight, Mr. Hames and I released simultaneous gasps. Then he clapped his thigh, grinning like a madman. "Your mom is terrifying," he told me, and turned to the class. "I'm calling a vote. All for Tarynn as the *Calypso*'s first officer?"

Everyone raised their hands.

Even India.

And me.

Tarynn smirked, self-assuredly. "I humbly accept this responsibility."

"Surprise, surprise," I said, but truthfully, that was pretty masterful manipulation. Which . . . might not bode well in an elected official.

Mr. Hames clapped his hands. "Then it's settled. That field study program was a stroke of genius. If you can get a meeting set up, I'll happily chat with your mom about it."

"I'll coordinate everything," Tarynn said with a confident smirk.

"Perfect!" He gestured toward the gaping expanse of Hangar 42. "Okay, let's go, let's go! We've got a starship to fix."

6

THE CREW OF THE *CALYPSO*

As a Tracker starship, the *Calypso* had a few defining characteristics. The first was its shape: a bulbous, bullet-like appearance with smooth lines and lights that glimmered like fireflies from the botanarium. The second was its standard engine, which wasn't something to sneeze at *before* Mr. Hames replaced it with a Starkwil slipstream generator. The third was its clean, minimalist interior.

When we crested the staircase into Mr. Hames's starship, I gaped, wondering what went wrong.

The place was trashed. Not in a smelly, moldy-food, or gross -unwashed-gym socks kind of way. More like Mr. Hames collected a souvenir from every place he visited, despite running out of room like fifty-six destinations ago. The cargo bay was about thirty feet tall, longer than any of Azura's classrooms, and there was still barely any floor space.

Mr. Hames kicked a massive beanbag chair out of the way, shoving it into the corner as best he could. "Come on in, come on! Plenty of room."

"For who? Us, or this junk?" Rhett sneered, tugging at his crisp shirt.

Mr. Hames blushed, rubbing the back of his neck. "You don't

have to be mean. It's a bit . . . unorganized . . . but there's space for everyone!" At his beckoning, the rest of the class filed in behind us with varying degrees of excitement. Tarynn, for example, seemed horrified, nudging what looked like a mechanical lizard with her foot, while India was positively gleeful.

"Stars, this is the coolest place," she gushed, grabbing my arm. I allowed myself to be tugged along as she knelt beside a collection of potted plants. One had polka-dot leaves, and she reached for it. "Max, look at this! Where's this one from, Mr. Hames?"

"Ah!" He hastily intercepted us, whisking the plant off the ground and setting it on a shelf well above our reach. "That's from Loconot. And unless you want liquefied eyeballs, you won't touch or otherwise inhale its aroma."

Good thing Mom was busy right now. I smirked. "Wow. This place seems super safe."

Mr. Hames rolled his eyes. "I wasn't expecting visitors. You telling me your room is much cleaner?"

"Yes." Across the cargo bay, Tarynn crossed her arms.

"Of course it is." Mr. Hames scrubbed his eyes with his palms.

India snickered, her dark gaze already roaming the large space for something else to admire. Something else from a foreign planet or a weird space station that would be inherently different from anything we found on Azura, just because it wasn't built at home, with love.

I tried not to appear as irritated as I felt, watching the fascination in her eyes. It didn't work. As Mr. Hames intercepted Nashira when she bent to examine what looked like a caged animal—"Ah, n-no, not that! Don't stick your fingers in there!"—India poked my shoulder.

"You look like you're sucking on a lemon, Max. Considering you begged me to set off that smoke bomb just to get a closer look at this ship, you should be more excited."

Well, I'd hardly *begged*. My lips pressed into a thin line, and I shoved my hands into my pockets. "It's just junk. If anything, it proves he has an unhealthy obsession with buying things he doesn't need."

India stopped short, turning to face me fully. The rest of our class had spread around the cargo bay, and Mr. Hames was bouncing from kid to kid, trying desperately to keep everyone from getting maimed or worse. But in that moment, it felt like Azura had stopped spinning, like we were suspended together, alone, far from here.

"You're upset that I want to leave," she said.

I stiffened. "No. Why would I care about that?"

"Because we've been friends since we were five, and I'm awesome," she replied, matter-of-fact.

"Modest too."

"It's a curse." She flipped her short hair with a flourish.

I laughed, but it sounded kind of sad. "It's stupid. Not like you're leaving anytime soon. Just—you never talked about it before now." My gaze flicked to Mr. Hames, and an irrational anger surged into my throat. "You never talked about it before *him*."

India glanced at our substitute teacher, then shrugged. "Well, he seems like he has some stories." Her expression turned wistful.

"Our lives are so boring on Azura. Don't you want adventures too?"

"How is setting off smoke bombs or breaking into cargo bays boring?" I demanded. "Seems like an adventure to me."

She sighed. "Never mind."

"Fine, yeah. Never mind," I said, just because I wanted to get the last word. Irritation curdled in my gut as I stomped away from her, catching Mr. Hames's attention with a wave of my hand. "Where's the engine room?"

"You can't leave yet," Tarynn—who'd climbed on a metal crate to reach Mr. Hames's height, therefore towering over the rest of us—snapped. "We're doling out jobs. It's a team effort."

"A crew effort," Mr. Hames said helpfully. "Let's see. Basic positions: navigator, communications, tech support, medic, cook. And mechanic." He beamed, nodding at me. I frowned in response, but he didn't notice.

"And first officer," Tarynn reminded him. She was still standing on the metal crate, and she ticked something on a holopad. I was puzzling through where she'd gotten a hold of one of those until I saw Louisa fidgeting uncomfortably in her shadow.

Ah. Our lovely class president, everyone.

"What's a navigator do?" India asked from the other side of the small crowd.

I steadfastly ignored her, as if I couldn't care less.

Mr. Hames bounced on his toes. "Oooh. Great question. The navigator navigates."

"Descriptive," she drawled.

He chuckled, rubbing his neck. "When the captain decides

to travel somewhere new, the navigator enters the coordinates, then ensures the ship stays on track. Kind of like a Galactic Positioning System."

"Doesn't the ship have one of those?" I asked.

"Well, yeah. But machines have to be told what to do," Mr. Hames replied.

India scowled at me, then said, "I want that job."

I scowled back, but she'd already turned away.

Tarynn made another note, then glanced at Louisa. "And obviously, Louisa's our tech support. Right?"

"Right." Mr. Hames beamed at her. Louisa shrank behind Tarynn, pushing her glasses up her nose, face reddening.

"And I'm communications," Nashira said, with enough force that she must have been dying to reiterate it this entire time. She fumbled in her backpack, and I half expected her to pull out Echo, even though I knew she didn't have the bat-like creature today. Instead, she produced one of her comm-phones. "I'm great with radio protocol!"

Tarynn nodded, tapping that into the holopad. "And Arsenio is the medic, I guess."

Rhett sneered. "Hope he doesn't try to injure us, just to have something to do."

Arsenio's fingers fluttered against the *Surgical Simulator* disc in his pocket. With his eyes downcast, he mumbled, "That's against the Hippocratic Oath. I wouldn't *do* that."

He looked pretty miserable, and I felt another pang of guilt for my earlier irritation. Apparently, he just wanted to be prepared in case something happened—which was honestly the sign of a good doctor.

Mr. Hames frowned at Rhett, but I spoke up before he could. "Pretty big words for someone who's going to be our designated chef."

"I'm making the uniforms, Max," Rhett snapped.

"I have a nutribot, so we don't *need* a chef. Rhett, how about steward?" Mr. Hames suggested. "They handle the needs of the crew, mostly in the clothing department."

Rhett examined his perfectly manicured nails and shot me a scowl. "Sounds like a job for a *true professional*." He spoke the words like they were so creative, even though that "true professional" line was plastered all over the Resnik Clothing Shop on the market level.

In the corner, Louisa raised her hand.

Mr. Hames pointed at her. "Yes?"

"C-can I still cook?" she asked quietly.

Nashira flounced over, throwing an arm around her twin. "Oooh, her baking is legendary here. You'll see."

"If that brings you joy, the galley's all yours," Mr. Hames replied, and Tarynn made another note on Louisa's holopad.

Louisa beamed.

"Then that's that!" Our teacher clapped his hands. "Let's finish the tour, and then we'll get to work, hmm? Just don't touch anything yet. I need a night to—ugh—*clean*." On his tongue, the word sounded as poisonous as the plant from Loconot. He even accompanied it with a shudder. I swallowed a chuckle and moved to nudge India, only to realize she was still on the other side of the cargo bay.

Disappointment settled like a lump in my stomach, and I fell in line behind Mr. Hames as he began his tour.

The *Calypso* wasn't terribly big, by starship standards. Only one corridor branched from the cargo bay, and it led to a mess hall boasting two lunch tables. Across from the kitchen, there was a spiral staircase to the second deck, paired next to a ladder descending into the floor. That would take me to the engine room, no doubt.

But we went up instead. The spiral staircase opened to a thin hallway with four crew rooms, each with two bunks, and the captain's quarters. Past those, there was an observation deck that wrapped around the nose of the bullet-like starship, with big windows and three plush couches. Near the observation deck, another ladder drew my attention: the path to the flight deck. While the other kids plopped onto the couches, buzzing with conversation, Mr. Hames addressed those of us looking at the ladder with interest.

"Only a few in the flight deck at a time. It's fairly small."

India leapt at the chance.

I, however, was still annoyed. So, even though Dad had always said Tracker starships had the most intricate flight decks, I turned away, stalking back through the mess hall to the other ladder, the one leading into the belly of the ship.

The engine room.

Alone, I landed in the space with a thump. It was deceptively big, spanning nearly the whole length of the *Calypso*, lined with pipes and tiny plastiglass windows. Against the back wall, a bank of three standard-sized escape pods caught my attention. Nestled in the middle was a docking station for rogue escape pods, required by intergalactic law in case the *Calypso* was pinged with an SOS.

And there, in the center of the engine room, was the Starkwil generator. My breath caught. It was better than Dad had described. Better than the holovids I'd seen.

In person, it was *beautiful*.

It looked like an itty-bitty star, a soft-blue orb that illuminated the entire space. Actually, "star" wasn't too far off; Starkwil had patented the Cosmiton technology, which basically took the energy of a star and squished it way, way down, then channeled the power into a starship's mainframe to propel it through space at frightening speeds.

Mr. Hames's generator hovered in the center of a circular panel, appearing almost serene. But looks were deceiving. One wrong move, and all that energy could consume Azura and kill us all.

Which was why I wrinkled my nose at a set of tools discarded on the floor nearby. Mr. Hames, tinkering with his starship without a clue what he was doing. If Mr. Keller saw this, he'd blow a gasket.

I mean, to be fair, if he knew *I* was trying to fix it, he'd blow two.

But all slipstream generators attached to their host starships the same way: with cables and circuitry. If this was really a problem with the generator itself, the orb wouldn't be glowing blue;

it'd be exploding. And everything below it, the circular panel and the wires and the hardware? That, I could handle.

"Figured I'd find you down here," a voice from behind me said. I jumped, whirling to see Mr. Hames at the base of the ladder. He held up his hands, laughing a little. "Sorry. Didn't mean to startle you. Tarynn and Rhett are getting uniform measurements, but I noticed you'd left, so I figured—" He paused, rubbing his arm. "What do you think?"

"I think it's broken," I replied.

He flinched, and I felt kind of bad for being so blunt. But he circled around me, stopping to gaze at the generator like a proud parent. "It took me seven years to save for this. Seven *years*. Every digit that wasn't going to food went straight into this thing."

"Can't have been that hard, when you owned your own ship."

"What, the *Calypso*? It wasn't mine. Not back then." He stared at the ceiling, as if recalling a painful memory. "It belonged to an old friend. Another wha—ah, another explorer."

He'd cut himself off. He was about to say something *truthful*, and then he'd lied instead. I wanted to pull apart his words, stop the secrecy, but he must have seen the look in my eyes. Instead, he said, "So you used to fix starships with your dad? That's interesting."

He'd changed the subject to *that*? Defensiveness prickled along my spine, and I muttered, "Not really."

"It is." Mr. Hames leaned against the bulkhead wall. "My father and I were never close, but I wish we had a relationship like that. I bet your dad would be really proud of you."

Cold fury bristled. How dare Mr. Hames, this *stranger*,

assume he would know anything about Dad? They'd never met. Dad loved Azura. He'd never have traveled the galaxy when he could have been right here, with Mom and me. As far as I was concerned, Dad had nothing in common with this man.

I couldn't keep the venom from my tone. "Well, he died. So I guess we'll never know."

"Max—"

"No, you don't get to talk about him," I snarled, angry tears pricking my eyes. I swiped them away. "You don't know me. Stop pretending like you care, when all you need is for me to fix your stupid ship." I kicked the panel around the Starkwil generator, feeling sick satisfaction when Mr. Hames gasped and surged forward.

Way to prove me right.

Fists trembling and eyes burning, I climbed the ladder and stormed out of the *Calypso*.

7

A LIBRARY OF KNOWLEDGE

At the central elevators, a familiar voice shouted, "Wait, Max! I'm coming."

India. I stuck my hands in my pockets but dutifully held the lift for her. No matter how annoyed I'd been, after what happened with Mr. Hames, it was kind of nice to see her sprinting after me. No one liked being sad and alone. At least, I sure didn't.

She slid into the lift, missing a step as the gravity lost focus. Since artificial gravity took more energy than the centripetal force of a spinning space station, they weren't typically used in tandem. A starship like the *Calypso* would use artificial gravity, but only after leaving the confines of Azura.

Of course, that just reminded me of Mr. Hames and his stupid broken generator and his stupid, thoughtless conversation starters. As the doors closed, I faced the panel of buttons so India wouldn't see the downturn of my lips, the red that probably rimmed my eyes.

"What happened?" she asked as I shoved the button for the eighth floor: the civil center. "I thought you were fixing the starship. Why'd you leave?"

"Mr. Hames said I could go."

"Liar," she replied wryly.

Never got much past her. I pursed my lips. "He brought up my dad. Talked like he knew him, and it—I don't know. It made me mad."

"Oh." For a long moment, silence stretched between us as the lift descended. India cleared her throat and changed the subject. "So, the civil center? We paying a visit to Tarynn's mom?"

I mock-shuddered. "Stars, no." The elevator doors dinged open, and we pushed off the back wall in unison, diving into the empty hallway leading toward the outer ring. "I want to check out the library."

India blinked, finding her footing as gravity returned. We weren't far from our destination—nothing was that far on Azura—but we still moved cautiously, in case one of the meandering adults thought to question why we weren't in class. "We researching something?"

"Some*one*," I replied, with a bit too much venom.

India grinned. "Finally cracking the elusive Mr. Hames, huh?"

For a moment, it was back to our version of normal, picking targets and causing mayhem. Like our disagreement—okay, okay, *argument*—never happened. Nothing like a common enemy to unite people.

I smirked. "You got it."

The library on Azura was fairly small. We all heard stories of old Earth libraries filled with paper books, but that was a luxury we couldn't afford on Azura. Instead, our library was dedicated to student research, with e-books for reference and display discs to download any pertinent images.

Although Azura had a reliable local network to handle

in-station communication, access to the Galactic Network was trickier. Space was *big*, so tapping into that signal took equipment beyond what a mere holopad could do. (Unless you were Louisa. Thanks to her scary impressive hacking skills, her holopad was airtight.)

Luckily, five years ago, Mayor Zhang had invested in a few top-notch computers with fairly decent hypernet speeds. They were behemoths, taking up half the library floor for just six machines, which meant we could use them to hide from old Mr. Krad, the librarian probably since Azura was founded. Maybe longer.

Huh. He and Mrs. Smith probably had loads to talk about.

When the library door slid open, he peeked over his desk. But his eyes were going, and he refused the surgery adults could get to fix them. We used that to our advantage, ducking behind the wooden desk before he realized it wasn't a malfunctioning door sensor.

After a moment of holding our breaths, Mr. Krad went back to his e-book. India and I grinned at each other, waited another beat, then crept away from his desk. As always, we made a bee-line for the machine farthest away. Sufficiently hidden from the librarian's prying eyes, we crammed together on one chair and powered it on.

"G-search 'Mr. Hames,'" India suggested as I navigated to the Galactic Search.

"His first name's Milo, remember?" I whispered back, and keyed the name onto the holographic keyboard. The search retrieved millions of documents, which hovered in the air around us, visible only to those sitting directly in front of the computer. At least we knew Mr. Hames wasn't lying about his name.

Of course, that didn't solve the question we both settled on.

"What's a *whaler*?" India breathed.

"I don't know." But there were at least sixty results within easy reach that emphasized the word. Everything from news articles from the inner planets to amateur photographs of deep space to passenger manifests to tracking logs.

My mind flashed back to Mr. Hames's earlier slip. *"Another wha—ah, another explorer."* He must have been about to say "whaler."

But what *was* that?

After a moment's thought, I tapped the nearest result, a display from the Interstellar Xeno-Biological Museum on Tephlon. It was a VR exhibit, a promotional thing from the museum to gather visitors. The other results faded away as a holographic gallery settled around us. As long as we sat perfectly still on the chair, it was as if we were perched in the museum itself.

India grinned like I'd given her the keys to the *Calypso*. She loved VR. I sat back and let her maneuver our image, zooming us closer to the object in question: a massive organic fin preserved in some kind of glass chamber.

It was huge, towering at least forty feet above our chair in the simulation. Even in the holographic light, the leathery skin shimmered like a backdrop of stars. My jaw dropped. "What kind of animal is *that* from?" If that was just one fin, the creature itself must be enormous.

India squeaked in excitement, pulling us closer to the

informational plaque beside the chamber. She read: "'Proposed fin of the *Stella Cetacea*, or star whale. Discovered in 2795 GS by famed astro-explorer Flandius Scoot, this fin is the only indication of life between the stars.'" For a moment, she was silent, her dark eyes flicking back to the chamber housing the fin.

Upon closer inspection, I realized the glass chamber was actually a pressurized vacuum, mimicking the harsh reality of space. The fin itself seemed to shine, almost like it had a layer of slime coating it. I put a hand on the holographic image, and it flickered a bit.

India laughed. "It's gotta be a hoax, right? Nothing lives in space."

Mr. Hames's comment yesterday flashed in my mind: *"Oh, you have no idea."* We'd all rolled our eyes, but—what if we were wrong?

We needed to do more research. Quickly, I waved my hand, pulling us out of the simulation. The search results appeared once again, tiling around us like a holographic dodecahedron. Holding my breath, I scanned the headlines of the nearest articles.

"Cruise Ship Passengers Claim to See Dark Shape in Space. Has Stella Cetacea Finally Resurfaced?"

"The True Implications of Star Whales: How Discovering the Galaxy's Most Elusive Creature Could Revolutionize Space Travel."

"Nearly Three Hundred Years Later, Whalers Are Still Hunting for the Mythical Stella Cetacea."

"I don't think Mr. Hames thinks it's a hoax," I said. "And he's not alone. According to this, there are thousands of whalers roaming the galaxy." My hands stilled on one particular headline: *"Scientists or Poachers? The Ethical Dilemma of Hunting for Star Whales."*

"Poachers," I repeated, brows furrowing. "Like Mrs. Smith was teaching us before Mr. Hames took our class. Remember? And Mr. Hames clearly isn't a scientist, so . . ."

India wrinkled her nose. "That's pretty awful."

"Well, this assumes these creatures actually exist, which is a pretty big stretch," I replied, pulling another article for her examination with the pinch of my fingers. "Look. It was a big movement three centuries ago, when the fin was first discovered. But other than claims of sightings, no hard evidence has been found."

She rolled her eyes. "Come on, Max. Drop the engineering bit and pull out your musical side. Imagine the possibilities! A massive whale swimming in space—"

I cut her off with a strangled choke. "Wait, what did you say?"

"A whale swimming in space . . . ?"

And for the second time, that memory slammed into me, hard enough to make my head spin. Because what had Dad said to Mom, just weeks before he died?

"I saw it again."

"Just floating in space, hmm?"

"Not floating, Camille. Swimming!"

My mouth went dry, even as my palms began to sweat. This couldn't be true. There weren't whales in space. But thinking critically, the evidence didn't lie. Dad wasn't the only one who'd "seen" something in the asteroid belt. For decades, Azuran miners spread rumors of songs in space, haunting melodies traveling where sound couldn't exist. Of asteroids moving drastically from day to day, outside their normal orbit—almost as if something had pushed them aside.

We were raised on these stories. Although usually they were twisted into cannibalistic space sirens that hunted disobedient children, but . . . every tale stemmed from somewhere.

India raised an eyebrow. "Are you dying? You look like you're dying."

"What if Mr. Hames didn't wind up here by accident?" I murmured, gazing at the whaler headlines. "I thought his ship just broke down, but what if he was always heading to Azura?"

"Pretty sure he wouldn't have damaged his own ship just to visit us," India said.

Well, that was true. If his desperation for his stupid slipstream generator was any indication, he treasured that starship more than anything. And obviously, being stuck here was grating on him, if he'd resorted to asking a bunch of kids for help.

"Okay, well, maybe that was real," I admitted. "But this is why he's so desperate to fix his ship. He doesn't want to be on Azura. He wants to be out *hunting* these whales." Even just saying it left a bad taste in my mouth. If the star whales existed, they deserved better than a bunch of greedy poachers prowling the galaxy for them.

Even if they were good at hiding.

Still, it made me wonder how Flandius Scoot got a hold of that fin three hundred years ago. Did he try to capture an innocent whale, only to have it escape, slicing off a massive body part in the process? The thought made me shudder.

India had returned her attention to the search results for Mr. Hames. She waved aside the articles about whaling, tapping on a series of photographs instead. With a grin, she enlarged an image so the picture was almost as big as we were. It was a group portrait of about a hundred people crammed into the cargo bay of a much larger ship. It didn't look like the *Calypso*, but in the front row, plain as day, was Mr. Hames.

"Eww, look. It's Mr. Hames as a teenager." India jabbed a finger at our substitute teacher. "Look at the acne! And those clothes. What a nerd." She giggled, elbowing me to get in on the joke.

"So weird." I laughed, but my eyes scanned over the rest of the picture. There was a guy with thin blond hair and the beginnings of a mustache, his arm thrown around Mr. Hames's shoulder. Mr. Hames was maybe fifteen, and the other guy seemed a few years older. I studied their faces. "Looks like he's been a whaler for ages."

"Well, look at the date," India said. "Eighteen years ago."

We cycled through more of the photographs, pictures of the crew of this mysterious starship. On the fourth one, we discovered it was called the *Enrapture*, one of a fleet of whaler ships. Most of the other pictures didn't have Mr. Hames in them until we hit about the fifteenth photo. Three teenagers were leaning over an old slipstream generator, laughing hard enough they had tears in their eyes: Mr. Hames, mustache guy, and—

"Oh. Wait. Is that . . . ?" India's mouth dropped open.

I sucked air in, barely a gasp as my entire world changed. *Stars*, he looked so young back then! He must have been just a few years older than I was now. But his curly hair was a dead giveaway, and smiles never change.

I stared at the picture.

And my dad stared back.

8

THE TRUTH ABOUT
STAR WHALES

The *Calypso* was startlingly quiet when I stomped up the staircase into the cargo bay. I barely noticed, but India paused a few steps behind me, then said, "Ah. Lunchtime. No wonder I'm starving."

"Go eat, then," I replied distantly. Everything felt numb now. I'd burned a copy of the photograph onto a tiny display disc, and my fist clenched around it almost painfully. For something so tiny, it dug an awfully huge hole in my heart.

Dad hadn't stayed on Azura all his life. He told me he'd never left. He and Mom got married young, and they had me shortly after. Between that and school, there wasn't *time* for him to travel on this random starship, with these random whalers.

But the evidence was cutting into my palm.

With everything I thought I knew collapsing into lies, I turned to the one person I could still yell at. I stopped in the middle of the cargo bay and bellowed, "Mr. Hames!"

It was rude, obnoxious, and if Mom heard me shouting at an adult like this, she'd ground me for a week. Then again, *she'd* lied to me too. According to her, the Belmonts were Azuran people, with "the oxygen of this space station running through our veins."

I was sick of people lying to me.

So when Mr. Hames came jogging down the hallway from the mess hall, my blood boiled. He was holding a guitar—*no*, a decivox—and his smile was bright and ignorant, as if nothing was wrong, as if he hadn't been insincere this whole time.

Somehow, that just made me angrier.

"Oh, Max! Glad you're back. India told me your decivox is broken, so I found—"

"Why didn't you tell me you knew my dad?"

He blinked, taken aback. The decivox lowered as he realized we weren't having that conversation right now. My eyes flicked to the instrument: it was made of dark wood, nothing as pretty as Dad's, but still a gorgeous piece. But the rush of excitement at seeing one in mint condition was muted by my desperate need for answers.

"Did I? I don't think—Belmont . . . ?" He pressed his lips into a thin line, eyebrows screwing together. Like he was digging deep into the memories of the past, really trying to remember. Like he'd break something if he thought much harder.

I didn't care. "You knew him. Stop lying to me!"

India put a hand on my arm, her tone wary. "Max, that picture is pretty old."

"What picture?" Mr. Hames frowned.

I shook her off, scowling as I thrust the display disc at him. He took it with his free hand and pressed the button to activate it. The holographic picture flickered over the device, and his eyes widened as he stared at my dad. There was no denying this evidence.

My voice was cold, hard. "Looks like you and him were airtight. It *looks* like you guys were best friends. And then you come here and pretend you don't even know him!"

Didn't even know him. Tears burned my eyes.

Mr. Hames's expression lightened, and he laughed. "Oh my *stars*. Where did you kids find this?" Then he seemed to realize his tone, because he cleared his throat, sobering. "Hang on, though. I knew him, but his last name definitely wasn't Belmont. Damian, ah . . . Mendez. Montiguez . . . ?"

"Mendoza?" I offered weakly.

He snapped his fingers. "That's the one. Damian Mendoza."

It took the air from my lungs. That was Dad's original last name, before he married my mom and took hers. Which meant Mr. Hames was telling the truth. I'd come in here, screaming and ranting, but he really hadn't made the connection before now. How could he?

"And really, Kingston—um, Kane Kingston—was friends with him, not me," Mr. Hames added. "I was just a runner. *They* worked with the engineers. Ah, not to say he wasn't a great guy! Just that, aside from a few moments here and there, we didn't really hang out. He left a few months after I got there; something about missing a girl on some blackspace station—" He cut himself off, as if realizing just now where that space station was. His face went red with embarrassment, and he handed me the photo. "Ah, back here, I guess."

I stared numbly at my dad, laughing like he didn't have a care in the world. My hand shook. "Oh."

"I'm really sorry, Max," Mr. Hames said quietly. "But I promise I wouldn't lie to you."

And that infuriated me all over again. How could adults do that? Stare at a kid and say something when it obviously wasn't true?

"You already lied about being a whaler!"

The instrument in Mr. Hames's hand was being held so loosely, I thought it might crash to the ground. Beside me, India pressed her lips into a firm line. Muffled conversation was coming from the hangar—our classmates returning from lunch, but for this moment—it was just me and India and Mr. Hames.

"Why didn't you tell us the truth from the start?" India asked.

Our substitute teacher rubbed the back of his neck. "I wasn't lying. I just—whalers don't have the best reputation. I've been kicked out of places for being honest."

"Well, *yeah*. You're hunting innocent creatures," she said, hurt. She'd been so enamored with the idea of travel, but now she looked at Mr. Hames in disgust. "You're, like, a poacher."

He flinched. "No, no! You have it all wrong. I mean, some whalers are like that. But not me! I'd never kill a *stella cetacea*. That's why I left the *Enrapture* in the first place, just a few months after your dad did!" He clasped his hands, expression pleading. "Max, India. You have to believe me. That starship, Kingston and those whalers, they're in it for the money. But searching for these creatures is my life."

"If you're not looking for digits, then why waste your time?" I demanded.

"The *discovery* of it." Mr. Hames swept his hands into the air. The decivox hummed a bit as his fingers ghosted over the hollow space in the center, but it fell silent when he adjusted his grip. "Stars, kids! You can't even imagine how majestic they are. How breathtaking. It's like—like the entirety of space comes alive, just to cheer as they swim past. All I've ever wanted is to see them again. Just once more."

"Wait." I took a step forward. Behind us, Tarynn and Rhett crested the stairs, followed by the rest of our class. They fell silent as I said, "You've actually *seen* one?"

Mr. Hames glanced at them, then addressed me, desperately. "That's the reason the *Enrapture* gave me work in the first place. Your dad and I, we were the only people on that starship to have actually seen one."

I swallowed. Was that why Dad decided to leave Azura when he was younger? Did the whales really mean so much to him?

Mr. Hames continued, "I was seven and caught a glimpse of one near Tephlon. And your dad . . . he was in the asteroid belt just outside Azura. The captain of the *Enrapture* spent ages scouring Tephlon, since that's where Flandius Scoot's fin is housed. Thought maybe the one I saw was a friend visiting the resting place of its kin. But the captain didn't spend more than a few days around Azura. Even after your dad left, we kept looking in the wrong spot."

He trailed off, hanging his head. "I just want to see them

again. Just to know I didn't imagine it. But now I'm stuck here, and we're running out of time."

"Out of time?" I repeated, and he stiffened. Irritation spiked. Caught him in *another* lie. "What's the rush?"

Mr. Hames swallowed. "I mean, traveling the universe is expensive. Not a waste, of course. Travel is never a waste, but it's hard to make money when you can't even afford to staff a crew." He gestured helplessly around the belly of the *Calypso*. "Azura is kind of my last hurrah."

India and I exchanged a glance.

Behind us, Tarynn joined the conversation. She said, loudly, "What's going on? What are you trying to find?"

Mr. Hames sighed. "It doesn't matter. I'm stuck here, just like you guys. Here, Max." He handed me the decivox and the display disc, his tone utter melancholy. "India said you might like this. Something to play until you can send yours out for repair." With a forced smile, he strolled past Tarynn and the others, down the stairs. "Come on, kiddos. Let's get back to Classroom 7."

The rest of the class stared at me, some in shock, some in irritation. Somehow, I'd gone and ruined the one chance we all had at an adventure. Guilt churned, and my eyes dropped to the decivox in my hands. At the disc pressed between my palm and the dark wood of the instrument. I imagined Dad, laughing with his friends over a decade ago.

All this time, I'd thought Dad played it safe, stayed where everyone knew his name, where his future was carefully mapped. But it wasn't true. He was an adventurer, not much older than me when he left Azura to gallivant around the Fifth Star System searching for a mythical creature.

He'd *seen* these star whales.

And now I had the chance to follow in his footsteps.

"Mr. Hames, wait!" I called, and he stopped at the base of the stairs. I hesitated, then said, "Don't we have a slipstream generator to fix?"

And the smile on our teacher's face was brighter than a hundred suns.

9

THE GHOST OF HAUNTED MEMORIES

The next day, Mr. Hames stepped into Classroom 7 with Tarynn at his side and a grin on his face. "Well, kids, we officially have permission." And he flourished a holopad with Mayor Zhang's signature. Tarynn grinned smugly as he added, "Our field study program is approved for two weeks. Which is—all the time we should need." He paused, eyes skimming over me.

Gaze hopeful.

I shrugged. Probably, I could fix the generator in two weeks, but it felt good to make him sweat.

He cleared his throat. "Anyway, thank your mom for me, Max. She apparently sent Tarynn's mom a message after we chatted, endorsing the project."

"Wow," India said.

"Yeah . . ." I replied, suspiciously.

Of course, working on Mr. Hames's ship meant we were firmly in her domain. I bet all the cameras in her office were tuned to Hangar 42 and the *Calypso*. I wondered if Mr. Hames realized how closely she'd be watching us.

Or if he cared.

When we all gathered our stuff and strolled toward the lifts, the kids in the other classrooms gawked at us. India shamelessly waved at Mrs. Smith, who narrowed her eyes and turned back to her class. We laughed and caught up with Mr. Hames, who was chattering on about the benefits of us exploring a real starship.

Almost like he was buying into the lies he told my mom and the mayor.

None of us corrected him. Even *I* had to admit this was a pretty cool way to spend class.

We moved fast after that, and the week slipped by as we fell into our roles. India, Nashira, and Louisa settled into the *Calypso*'s flight deck, with India learning the navigational equipment, Nashira working on communications, and Louisa managing the onboard computer. Arsenio slid into the medbay like he'd always lived there. Rhett sized us for uniforms, which he produced by the week's end: faux-leather jackets and plain black pants that, I admit, made me feel like part of a real crew.

Meanwhile, Tarynn was living up to her title of Utterly Annoying. If she was nosy as class president, it was nothing compared to the agony we were subjected to by the *Calypso*'s controlling first officer.

During one particularly scathing encounter, India had interrupted Tarynn's most recent "progress check" to tuck a tiny blue-and-white marble into my jacket pocket. I was about to ask why I'd need a smoke bomb these days, but she'd stared right at Tarynn and said, "Just in case you need a quick getaway."

Tarynn rolled her eyes indignantly.

Mostly, though, I escaped the brunt of it, way down in the

engine room. Apparently, Tarynn was claustrophobic, and since the ladder leading to my domain was enclosed in a metal tube, it was too harrowing for her. That meant, whenever she could, India was downstairs with me, which usually earned her a scolding later on.

Or, in today's case, right now.

"India! I know you're down there," Tarynn bellowed. Her grating voice bounced off the tube walls, and we both flinched. "What kind of navigator are you? You're supposed to be in the flight deck."

"I'm the kind of navigator that takes a break when the ship isn't moving!" India hollered back.

I snickered, powering up my hydrodriver as I delved back underneath the Starkwil generator's circular console.

"Well, break's over," Tarynn pointed out. "This is class time, not social hour. Back to work!"

"I'm helping Max."

"Yeah, she's helping me. Very important maintenance work happening here."

For a moment, blessed silence. Everyone knew I was the essential one. Until the *Calypso* was up and running, the rest of our class was just goofing around. If I demanded a second pair of hands, our lovely first officer should provide me with such.

Tarynn knew it too. But a second later, her voice turned singsongy. "Oh, good, Mr. Hames. Tell India she's needed on the flight deck."

"Is she *actually* needed on the flight deck?" our teacher asked skeptically.

India held her breath. Even I paused my work to hear better. But Tarynn wasted no time in drawling, "Of course. We're running emergency drills, and she's the only one who hasn't practiced evacuations. Well, her and Max, but he's busy."

She didn't sound happy about it.

Mr. Hames's voice was louder; he was coming down the ladder. "Oh. Okay. India, if you don't mind?"

My best friend groaned, making it as loud and long-winded as possible. But when I mouthed, "Sorry," she just shrugged and whispered back, "Still better than class." Mr. Hames landed on the grated flooring, and she passed him with a wave.

When India's footsteps receded up the ladder, I pushed myself into a sitting position to address our substitute teacher. Since our argument over a week ago, he'd kept his distance; whatever he had to say now must be important.

To my surprise, he held a plate of cookies. From the smell, they were fresh, and definitely Louisa's recipe. My mouth watered, and he grinned. "Figured you might want a snack. You're working hard down here."

"It's fine," I replied, climbing to my feet to take one of the treats. "I like working on starships. Mr. Keller—the mechanic I usually work for—doesn't think I'm old enough to handle the big stuff." I set my jaw, smug satisfaction spreading through my veins. "Can't wait to tell him I repaired a generator he's never even seen."

Mr. Hames laughed, setting the plate on a nearby table before taking a seat on the floor beside the console. "I still feel bad. I wish I could help." He peered at the generator with interest, like a kid waiting to learn.

Like me, before Dad caved and gave me a hydrodriver and put me to work.

I took a bite of the cookie, letting the chocolate melt against my tongue. Louisa always used bittersweet chocolate, so her desserts were never too sugary. She also rarely made cookies, so the other kids must be going nuts. "Thanks," I said as an afterthought. "Nice of you to grab me some."

"Louisa's the one to thank," he replied, but his lips tilted into a smile nonetheless.

I wiped my hands on my black pants. Rhett had decided I wasn't allowed my leather jacket until I could "treat it properly," which basically meant doing mechanical work without getting grease everywhere. *Yeah, right.* Just to spite him, I'd stolen the jacket, then proceeded to mark it with all the grime I could find. He was furious, but I felt a lot better.

Mr. Hames studied the Starkwil generator while I polished off the cookie. "How's it going?"

I licked my fingers clean, scrubbed them on my pants, and rolled back under the generator's console. I was actually pretty close to finishing the repairs, but whenever an engineer promised that, some problem manifested. Like Dad always said, "Keep your mouth shut until the thing's running."

So I replied, "It's going."

Mr. Hames hummed affirmation, then said, "Well, I came down here to get a few voice recordings from you."

"Voice recordings?" I repeated.

"Yeah. When the *Calypso*'s fixed and we take it for a spin, we're going to need a cover in case anyone stops by Classroom 7—"

"Wait, wait. Take it for a spin?" I paused, twisting to stare at him through the winding mechanics of the console. He looked as confused as I felt, so I clarified, "We're going with you? For real?"

"I mean, I expected you all would. Do you want to stay on Azura instead?"

I'd honestly never thought that far ahead. I'd figured this was like when we were little kids playing smugglers-and-security: India and I would pretend to be something we weren't, have a bit of fun, and forget all about it by night's end.

That's what this was in my mind. Playing starship crew for two weeks. And once the *Calypso* was fixed, Mr. Hames would jettison into space and we'd be right back in Mrs. Smith's class.

But now Mr. Hames was fidgeting, plucking at a string on his pants as he waited for my reply. So I blurted, "I just assumed you were using us to fix your ship, and then—then you'd leave. For good."

"I thought about it," he admitted.

The truth. *Finally.*

He laughed self-consciously, running a hand through his red hair. "But, I mean, Azura isn't as bad as I thought. Your mom has been really nice. And this weekend, I played chess on the recreation level, and the old-timers let me win." He shrugged, grinning ear to ear. "I think I owe you an apology, Max. I misjudged this place. You've got a great community of folks here."

"Oh," I said, pride swelling at that admission. "So you think you're going to stay for a while?" I tried to keep my tone casual. *Just good gossip*, I told myself. *Not like you care.*

But a week in Mr. Hames's class had been more fun than anything with our old teacher, Mr. Bruska, the one getting physical therapy in the inner planets. And it was definitely more fun than Mrs. Smith's crotchety old classroom.

Mr. Hames was quiet for a moment. "I don't know. My main priority has to be the star whales. Everything else is secondary."

"Right," I said, too quickly. My hydrodriver locked onto a loose screw as I resumed reattaching a metal plate I'd removed earlier. "So, um, what do you need the voice recording for? I thought we had permission for the field study."

"Under the stipulation the airlock doors never open," Mr. Hames said, like he thought it was totally unreasonable.

"Mom's going to know the second we leave."

Mr. Hames glanced sideways, as if Mom was listening to us from way inside his ship. "That's why I'm having Louisa spoof the cameras. Did you know that girl can hack almost anything? She can make it seem like the airlock doors never opened, according to Camille's displays." He grinned mischievously.

It was weird that he was now on a first-name basis with my mom.

I quirked an eyebrow, swallowing another bite of the cookie. "So you want to fool people into thinking we're back in Classroom 7, even while we're touring the asteroid belt? That's a pretty flimsy disguise."

"Alone, sure," he agreed, and through the piping and cables, I could see the sly gleam in his eyes. "But Nashira's faking an exit report for the space traffic controller, so Kaito'll think we're just another mining ship unless he looks outside. Louisa's got the airlock situation handled. Tarynn and I took a holographic recording of the classroom too, so anyone peeking through the door's window will think we're really there. That's where the voice recording comes in; hours of real classroom discussion on a loop, just for anyone listening from the hallway."

Wow. My jaw dropped. "That's . . . elaborate. Respect, Mr. Hames."

He swelled at the praise. "Hey. I was a trickster too, back in the day. What's that saying? Better to beg forgiveness?"

We both laughed. For a moment, it was like we were actually friends, not just student and teacher. But then he cleared his throat and said, "Ah, have you tried that decivox yet? I hope it's not out of tune."

I went silent, attaching the last screw of that metal panel. The truth was, I hadn't touched the instrument he'd left perched by the escape pods. Not because I didn't have the time, but because whenever I looked at it, fear choked me.

I'd only played on Dad's decivox, with its broken rods and horrid sound. What if I tried the working one, and I wasn't any good?

"Max?" Mr. Hames asked.

"Not yet. I'll, um, get around to it." As an afterthought, I said, quietly, "But thanks. For finding that."

"India said you're a great musician," he replied curiously. "I would love to hear it. I played the guitar when I was your age, but it's been a while since I picked it up." Now he paused. "Been a while since I've focused on anything but the whales."

That sounded like a pretty sad existence. I didn't even think before saying, "That's a shame."

"It really is," Mr. Hames said, rubbing his chin. "Maybe you and I can put on a concert for the class. My guitar is around here somewhere." He'd cleaned up the dangerous junk after that first day, but his ship wasn't "tidy" by any means. I laughed, and he smirked. "Hey, don't judge a man by his mess. It's organized chaos."

"If you say so," I replied. "Mom would have a fit if she came in here."

He laughed. "She'd have more than a fit if she knew what we were planning. Now I know where the phrase 'mama bear' came from."

I'd never heard that line, but it seemed to fit Mom pretty well. I reached for a few more screws I'd undone hours ago. Mr. Hames dropped one in my hand, and I shimmied back under the console. "She wasn't always this bad. It's just because of—what happened to Dad." I tried to get through it without choking on the words, but that lump still swelled in my throat.

Mr. Hames's voice lowered, filled with . . . not pity, but sympathy? Sadness?

"What, ah, what happened to him? Can I ask?"

No. You can't. It's none of your business.

But he was staring, brows knitted like he actually cared, and it had been a long time since someone cared about Dad. So I answered, although my reply was mechanical, rehearsed. "He was working on a mineship near the asteroid belt, and it exploded. He barely made it back. F-freak accident, they said." I drew a few deep breaths. My eyes burned, but I still forced myself to add, "We don't talk about it."

It was a pointed hint, but Mr. Hames misconstrued it. "Ever? You and your mom don't talk about losing him?"

My breath hitched, and irritation sparked in my chest. He said that like Mom had failed me somehow, even though she was the only person in the universe who understood. "No. And I don't *want* to."

"Okay. You don't have to," he replied.

"Good."

Silence filled the engine room for several minutes, wherein I focused on the console and Mr. Hames didn't ask any more annoying personal questions.

It didn't last long. Soon, he sighed. "Listen, Max. I can't tell you what Damian was like on the *Enrapture*, but if you ever want to talk about him, or . . . or cry, I'll be here."

Who did Mr. Hames think he was? The very suggestion had my cheeks warming in anger, my hands trembling against the hydrodriver. "Why would I cry about him? It's been two years. We're all fine."

"I know," he backpedaled quickly. Pacifying me. He pushed to his feet, clearing his throat, even though I stubbornly refused to look at him through the empty spaces in the console. "It's just . . . talking helps me when I'm sad. I thought it might help you too."

"I'm *fine*," I snapped.

"Okay. Anyway, we'll do the voice recordings when you're

ready. Just come find me or Tarynn." He paused at the base of the ladder, even as I glared at the screw under my hydrodriver. "I'm sorry, Max. For everything. I wish I could help more." With a sigh, he left.

And as I sat under the console of the Starkwil generator Dad would have *loved* to see, alone except for the memories, tears leaked into my hair and a cold determination settled in my heart.

Mr. Hames may not know what Dad was like on the *Enrapture*, but he wasn't the only one in those pictures.

Kane Kingston was too.

And I knew just how to contact him.

10

A DISCUSSION WITH KANE KINGSTON

Two days later, India and I were walking to the cafeteria—"another stipulation of the field study program," Mr. Hames said with a long-suffering sigh, "like we don't have food on the *Calypso*"—when we ran into my mom.

Well, my mom and Dr. Drose. I stopped short, flinching on reflex when I sighted Arsenio's mom. They were strolling away from the cafeteria, and Mom was munching on an apple. I stopped walking, staring in disbelief. Apples were always Mom's dessert. If she was eating one of those, that meant she'd just finished lunch.

My eyes flicked to Dr. Drose, and disgust welled in my throat.

She was eating lunch with *her*.

The surgeon who didn't save Dad.

The betrayal hit hard, slamming me like a mineship to the face. India paused a few feet from me, asked, "Max?" and then followed my gaze. Her eyes widened, and she grabbed my arm. "Come on. It doesn't mean you have to talk to her—"

But that's when Dr. Drose noticed me. Her face froze, then rearranged into an expression of careful consideration. The same expression she'd worn when she broke the news about Dad.

I clenched my fists.

"Oh, Max. India." Mom glanced at the cafeteria, then smiled warmly. "You kids going to lunch?"

"Yep. In fact, they're waiting for us," India replied, and tugged my arm again.

Dr. Drose blinked. "Oh, are you talking about Arsenio? He was hoping to join you two someday. Talks about it all the time at home."

Mom glanced at her, brows knitted together, before glancing back at me. "That'd be nice. Why don't you invite Arsenio to your table?"

I stared at her. How—how could she ask me that? After everything the Drose family had ruined for us, how could she just expect me to be friends with Arsenio again? Why was she acting like that day in the hospital *never happened*?

Mom frowned. "Max?"

I had to get out of here. I let India tug me along, finally, and barely managed to say, "Whatever," before we bolted through the doors into the cafeteria. The din of conversation masked my buzzing anger, but I didn't miss how Mom squinted at me through the doors before turning back to Dr. Drose.

Then she laughed, just a little, like they were suddenly besties.

"You okay?" India asked.

I was shaking a bit. "I just—I don't understand."

"Get in line. Come on. Let's . . . well, get in line." Now India laughed, boisterously. Desperate to get back to normal, I laughed too, though mine was far weaker, more forced.

Luckily, India was a pro at redirecting conversations, because she chattered quietly about the upcoming expedition while we got our food and picked a table by the plastiglass windows. When Louisa appeared, things almost felt back to normal. She had her golden holopad in hand and waited quietly until we stopped talking.

"S-sorry to interrupt," she squeaked.

"Don't be sorry," India said, smiling brightly. She patted the seat beside her. "You can sit with us. We invited your sister earlier, but she brought Echo, and apparently microptera don't do well with cafeteria noise. And Tarynn and Rhett just laughed at us."

I snorted; we most assuredly did *not* ask those two for company. Just like we also didn't ask Arsenio. After what happened outside, I had no desire to interact with him ever again.

India tossed an arm over her forehead, dramatically. "We're kind of starved for attention right now. Rejection hurts."

Stars, this girl. I snorted, and India grinned.

Louisa ducked her head, pushing her glasses farther up her nose. "Actually, I'm not here for that."

"Ouch." India faked offense, pressing a hand to her heart. "*Louisa*. And here I thought we were friends. You, me, and Nashira against the world. The Flight Deckers."

"The Flight Deckers?" I repeated.

India laughed. "Too cool for you, Belmont. Don't get weird about it."

"Ouch," I echoed drily. We exchanged a grin, until Louisa cleared her throat again. She tapped something on her holopad, then turned the transparent screen to me.

"I just—Max. You wanted to know if anyone replied to that message."

I stiffened, the blood draining from my face. Beside me, India raised an eyebrow, curious and silent. But she faded away as I stood, taking hold of Louisa's holopad. Mr. Hames had discovered what we all already knew: that our resident computer nerd was quite the hacker. So competent, in fact, that she'd manipulated her own private holopad to have all the Galactic Network access Mr. Krad's library computers did.

Including hypernet communications.

The text scrolling before my eyes was impossible to misread. MESSAGE RECEIVED: KANE KINGSTON.

It worked. He really answered.

"What message?" India asked, squinting at me. Suspicion tinged her voice. "Max, who are you talking to?"

Louisa shifted, clearly uncomfortable. "It was pretty easy to find him. He's captain of the *Enrapture* now. I just sent the message you gave me, and he replied in a day. I didn't read anything, though! I know it's private." She blushed, removing her glasses to rub the lenses with her shirt. I caught a glimpse of a tiny gold chip embedded into the earpiece, which she whisked out of sight when she caught me looking. I'd never seen those frames for sale on Azura, but maybe her parents ordered them from the inner planets.

"*Who* are you talking about?" India demanded, frustrated now.

Much as I loved egging her on, this wasn't the time for a temper tantrum. I slid back into my seat, showing her the holopad . . .

and the name attached to the mysterious message. Her eyes widened. "Wait. Kane, as in, your dad's friend?"

"Best friend," I clarified. "His best friend as a teenager. That's what Mr. Hames said."

"Pretty sure Mr. Hames said Kane was 'better friends' with your dad than *he* was. Not that they were best friends." India frowned, her brows knitting together. Her concern was kind of annoying. "What are you hoping to gain from this, Max? It . . . it won't bring him back." The last sentence was barely whispered, but she set her jaw stubbornly.

I scowled. There was no way she wouldn't do the exact same thing, reach out to a stranger for details about what *her* dad was like as a teenager. Even if it was just a few sentences. Even if the stranger captained a starship of poachers.

I had to know.

But Louisa stood behind us, shifting awkwardly, so I didn't say that. Instead, I pressed my lips together. "Mr. Hames still isn't telling us the whole truth." When India opened her mouth, I interrupted, "You know it's true. 'Three weeks.' That's what he kept muttering that first day in our classroom. He's running 'out of time.'" I used air quotes so she'd remember our substitute teacher had said those exact words a week ago.

India pursed her lips. "I mean, I guess. But that doesn't mean he's some supervillain. There are lots of reasons an adult might have a deadline."

"Maybe he's dying," Louisa said. When we glanced over our shoulders at her, she turned bright red. "A-Arsenio said a lot of life-threatening diseases don't have symptoms."

"There you go." India tapped the table. "Add 'possibly dying' to the list. Point is, not everything is a plot to destroy us and everything we love. Sometimes, a quirky teacher is just a quirky teacher."

"I know," I said petulantly, returning my attention to the holopad. To the little message waiting to be opened and answered.

India peered closer. "Do you, Max? Because you've had it out for Mr. Hames since he got here. Why does he bother you so much?"

Wasn't it obvious? Because, for the first time in our lives, India wanted to leave Azura and travel the galaxy. Because the rest of the class adored him even though he lied. Because things were changing, and it was all his fault.

But mostly because of Dad. Because, even though I clearly didn't want to talk about the accident or the crippling emptiness in our weird two-person family, or Mom's aching tears whenever we were reminded of him—and we were *always* reminded of him—or the gaping black hole in my heart that might swallow me if I didn't *stop thinking about him*, Mr. Hames kept pressing.

He kept asking.

And whenever he asked, it took me that much longer to get back to the careful, unemotional existence I'd perfected before he arrived on Azura.

"He doesn't bother me," I lied.

India rolled her eyes. "If you say so, Max-a-million."

Louisa bounced on her heels. "Do you, um . . . need my holopad for much longer, Max? Because lunch is almost over, and Mr. Hames wants me to sync it to the *Calypso*'s computer."

I couldn't exactly read Kane's message with India prowling over my shoulder, judging me. And yeah, I was kind of scared of what he'd written. The last link to my father. . . . What if he didn't say what I wanted to hear?

What if he wasn't really friends with Dad?

It was easy, then, to power down the holopad and hand it back to Louisa. I studiously ignored India's skeptical gaze as I said, "No, it's fine. Thanks for telling me."

Louisa clutched the holopad like I'd given her back her arm— or her soul. Some people had teddy bears or blankets. According to Rhett, I had my hydrodriver. And Louisa had her holopad.

When she left, India raised an eyebrow at me. "I thought you'd want to read that message."

"Nah," I said, smiling brilliantly. Lying through my teeth. "You're right. Mr. Hames can have secrets. Doesn't mean he's a bad guy." Then I stole a carrot off her plate, and she was sufficiently distracted.

———————

Of course, after class, I wasted no time forging an excuse to get away. Since I had a perfectly usable decivox now, India and I hadn't been going to the abandoned storage room on the recreation level lately. But I had yet to play Mr. Hames's decivox either; it was new and weird, and just holding it felt like I was cheating on my dad's broken one, somehow.

Instead, most of our after-school hours were spent as a whole class, goofing around together. We'd always been acquaintances— it's impossible to be in a classroom with the same people for half a decade and *not* get to know them—but this was different, like we were suddenly all part of this secret club. Like we were actually friends now. Even I had to admit it was kind of cool.

But today wasn't like other days. Today, Kane Kingston was waiting. So, even though Tarynn declared we were all playing *Hutts' Heroes* VR until dinnertime, I ducked out almost immediately.

"Sorry, guys," I said, feigning embarrassment. "Mr. Keller's expecting me today."

It was a lie. I'd slowed down with Mr. Keller's shop since my school hours were now spent under the Starkwil generator. Hertz-rated infibrillators couldn't really compare. When I told Mr. Keller I was busy this week, the old man had just rolled his eyes and said, "Good. Go be a kid for once," and slammed the door in my face.

But everyone knew about my part-time job, so it was a fool-proof plan. Even India barely gave me a sideways glance as I waved goodbye and leapt into one of the central elevators. The second the doors closed, I pressed the button for the civil center.

The library was more crowded than usual, but a computer was still open. Mr. Krad ignored me as I filed inside and slid into the seat, powering on the machine. The holo-display came to golden life around me, and I opened the private messaging application, logging in with a few swift keystrokes.

MESSAGE RECEIVED: KANE KINGSTON was still exactly as I'd left it.

Holding my breath, I opened it, scanning the words from my dad's old friend.

Hey, kid!

Stars, I can't believe Damian went and got married to that girl after all. Sorry to hear he passed, but hey, sometimes bad things lead to new friends. After all, your dad and I were closer than the two moons of Hysteria. Happy to answer your questions!

PS: How's old Milo Hames, hmm? Haven't seen him since he joined that crazy kook on the Calypso. He still scouring the stars for those whales?

I blinked, surprised. Maybe the crew of the *Enrapture* weren't whalers anymore. It made sense; whaling clearly wasn't a lucrative business, if Mr. Hames couldn't afford to pay his own crew. A big ship like the *Enrapture*, with a crew complement of a hundred, would definitely have to dabble in something else.

But excitement surged as I reread his message. He wanted to talk. He was nice and excited, and he'd tell me anything I wanted to know! Finally, I'd get answers about Dad's life before marrying Mom.

Fingers trembling, I typed a reply on the holographic keyboard that shone on the computer's desk.

It took a good ten minutes to type all the questions I had, and it came out a garbled mess. But I was too excited to fix it.

Thanks, Mr. Kingston! I'd really love to know when my dad left Azura. How long was he on the Enrapture? Did he travel anywhere else before coming home? Did you ever hear him play the decivox? I found one in his closet two years ago. Was he any good? Which did he like better, engineering or music? And what about whaling? Was he trying to capture a star whale, or just study it?

PS: Mr. Hames is still hunting for them. Are you? He's hoping to find one in the asteroid belt near our space station, which is crazy.

I pressed Send, then stared at the inbox for a few minutes, as if Mr. Kingston might reply right away. Which was silly, since he was the captain of a huge starship now, so of course he'd be busy.

But just as I pushed out of the chair, ready to power down the computer and wait another day, a new message arrived. I plopped back into my seat, jaw dropping. He'd replied. So fast! Reading the first sentence, I could imagine him laughing, mustache bouncing with mirth.

Call me Kane, please. Mr. Kingston was my father. You've got a lot of questions, kid, but let's see. Your dad traveled on the Enrapture for maybe a month before catching a ride back to that space station. He practically begged to come with us, but he missed some girl back home. He'd play the decivox for us all the time, though. Damn talented, Damian was! But he loved engineering too. Guy was basically a brother to me. I'm gonna miss him.

But, kid, your last questions are . . . odd. Every whaler wants to capture a star whale, even your dad. Milo told you about the reward, didn't he? A government-issued grant of one million digits for anyone who brings undeniable proof of the star whales' existence. The money expires on the 300th anniversary of Flandius Scoot's discovery, just a week and a half from today. Hames always had absurd ideas, but I can't fault him for continuing the hunt. For me, I won't give it up until I'm dead in space!

I glazed over the rest of his message, zeroing in on the amount of money. My mouth went dry. A *one-million-digit* reward for capturing a star whale?

I typed back: *Why would the government offer a grant like that?*

Kane's reply was immediate and amused.

A whale in the vacuum of space. Think of what they could learn from something like that. Radiation-blocking capabilities for starships and suits. Propulsion tactics we can't even imagine. Creatures relate to their environment, so the star whales must affect space in ways we haven't discovered yet. Obviously, the government would want to know more.

"The government would want to know more." If Kane was equally curious, it was only under the shroud of a one-million-digit reward . . . because apparently that's what whalers cared about.

This had to be what Mr. Hames was hiding.

Why hadn't he mentioned the reward?

Well, probably because we'd just accused him of poaching. Irritation curdled in my gut. Another lie to save face. He was only "running out of time" because the deadline for this grant was fast approaching, and if he found a star whale after that, he wouldn't get any money for it. I clenched my fists, scowling at the message.

But another thought edged into my mind, quelling my anger. *Dad* had wanted the money too. Mr. Kingston—ah, Kane—said so, clear as the stars outside. And even if I didn't entirely trust Mr. Hames, I trusted that Dad would never have put an animal in danger for money. There had to be some method of capturing a star whale without hurting it, or Dad would never have entertained the idea of being a whaler.

Mr. Hames lied, but India was right. There was no reason to think he was a supervillain out to destroy an innocent creature.

It must be fine.

Swallowing my hesitation, I typed a sheepish reply to Kane. For now, I'd give them all the benefit of the doubt.

11

A SPACEWORTHY SHIP

Two days after that, around 9:00 a.m. Galactic Standard Time, I fixed the slipstream generator.

It happened by accident. I reattached one of the cables tethering the glowing orb to the circular console, and when it snapped into place, the entire starlike orb shifted from blue to purple. It was such a gradual change, I didn't notice until I emerged from the console, wiping my forehead with Rhett's precious leather jacket.

And then I yelped in excitement, heart hammering in my chest. *I did it.* The generator was working. My hydrodriver slipped from my fingers, and I descended on the circular panel, tapping buttons and twisting knobs to get it fully powered up.

There was no mistaking it. A soft rumble echoed through the engine room, and the whole ship began to vibrate. Soon after, the hammering of footsteps was impossible to ignore.

As expected, Mr. Hames slid down first, followed closely by India, Nashira, and Rhett. I froze, caught off guard. Our teacher's jaw dropped as he stared at the glowing purple orb. And then he started to laugh.

It didn't take long before we were all laughing with him, the pure happiness of accomplishment settling into our bones. India squeezed my shoulders, and Nashira clapped me on the back. Even Tarynn, peering down from the top of the ladder, was grinning.

"Oh, Max, you brilliant *genius*!" Mr. Hames exclaimed, and swept me into a spinning hug. I squirmed to get away, but he didn't hold on long, just enough to ruffle my hair before taking a closer look at the Starkwil generator. "Haven't seen it this color since I dropped my crew off at Lucarro XI. Gorgeous."

"Nice job, Max," Rhett, standing at the base of the staircase, said begrudgingly.

"Good thing I always have a hydrodriver as a 'security blanket,' huh?" I grinned. "By the way, these uniforms are *perfect* for mechanical work."

It was a direct dig, considering the leather jacket was too stiff to be comfortable and mine was smeared with grease. Rhett glared at me, but for the first time in our lives, he didn't respond scathingly. For the first time, I was more necessary than him.

Which basically made me untouchable.

India offered her elbow, which I tapped in accomplishment. We smirked at each other, right up until Mr. Hames clapped his hands.

"Okay, kiddos! Who's ready for our first excursion?"

"Wait," Tarynn called from the top of the ladder. "Right now? Mr. Hames, we're not ready to go yet. We need more preparation. Nashira's getting a hold of her uncle's patrol routes, and Louisa is still synthesizing the audio recordings."

Mr. Hames strolled to where Rhett was standing, glancing up at our first officer. "Come on, Tarynn. Where's your sense of adventure?"

She gaped. "I'm ready for adventure! I just think we should adventure *after* the weekend, when we're ready."

"We want to go now!" India exclaimed, taking hold of my arm. "Max didn't fix this thing to watch it break over the weekend."

"That's not how it works—" I started to say, but she cut me off with a squeeze of her hand.

Oh. *Right*. I nodded firmly, the corners of my lips tilting upward. "I mean, waiting might gum up the works. Then we're back at square one."

Mr. Hames saw right through it, but he flashed me a thumbs-up behind Rhett's back, even though I hadn't done it for him. But his voice was bright as always. "There. See, Tarynn? It's got to be today. Lesson number one: if you wait for everything to be perfect, you'll be waiting forever."

I frowned. No one else knew about his deadline, but after my running dialogue with Kane, it was painfully obvious Mr. Hames was desperate to get back into space, desperate to scour the asteroid belt for signs of a star whale.

Dad wanted to find one too, I reminded myself. And what Dad wanted, I wanted.

So, I kept my mouth shut.

And a few moments later, Tarynn huffed. "Fiiine. Louisa! Timeline's moved up. We're leaving now." Her footsteps receded down the hallway above our heads, and the other students climbed the ladder out of the engine room. Mr. Hames motioned for me to follow.

In the upstairs hallway, kids rushed back and forth. Louisa

was securing the kitchen galley, flipping red latches to keep the drawers and cabinets closed before plucking her holopad from her pocket. Nashira and India scaled the staircase, making their way to the flight deck with Louisa close behind. The Flight Deckers, reunited again.

Meanwhile, Tarynn and Rhett followed Mr. Hames as he inspected the exterior of the starship. With nowhere else to go, I climbed the staircase after India.

And promptly ran into Arsenio, just outside his medbay.

"Oh, h-hey, Max," he stammered. I forced a smile, because I still felt bad for how I'd snubbed him last week. He smiled back. "Congratulations on fixing the generator. Louisa told me everything's running normal now."

"Hopefully," I said. That swell of pride hit again, the certainty that I'd fixed something otherwise utterly broken. And here Mr. Keller didn't think I could handle anything bigger than an artificial gravity device. Ha. Joke's on him.

Arsenio hesitated, glancing over his shoulder. We were alone in the hallway, with six closed doors stretching beyond us: the *Calypso*'s crew rooms. At the end of the hall was the observation deck, brimming with comfy couches. Beside Arsenio was one more room—the medbay. I hadn't seen it during the tour, but it looked pretty intense.

Although he probably thought the same about the engine room.

"Did you need something, Arsenio?" I asked, trying to be polite. Somehow, it came off as annoyed.

He winced, his freckles bright against his skin. "Do you hate me, Max?"

"What?" I blanched. "Why would I hate you?"

But even that sounded forced.

Arsenio sighed, shoving his hands into his leather jacket's pockets. I hadn't noticed before, but he wore an apron over his black pants, with scissors and a tiny first aid kit poking from the depths. Rhett must have made it special for him.

"I know we were never as close as you and India, but I thought we were friends. You know, before."

Before my dad's accident. I pressed my lips into a firm line, trying to focus on the point at hand. "We were friends. *Are* friends."

"Mr. Hames thinks you might be mad at me," he said quietly. I bristled, and he held up his hands, hastening to reassure me. "Ah, not mad. He said you're sad, and angry, because of what happened. And since my mom operated on him, I'm an easy target. 'The embodiment of your grief,' he said."

What was he doing, talking to Mr. Hames about us? As if that nosy teacher had anything to do with life on Azura. As if the decaying friendship of his mechanic and his medic meant anything to the functionality of this starship.

"Mr. Hames is wrong," I snapped. "I'm not angry."

Arsenio shrank into himself, and I realized I'd moved forward, clenching my fists threateningly. Shocked, I pressed against the opposite wall, putting distance between us. As if it might add distance to this conversation.

It didn't. Arsenio swallowed hard. "She cried for days, Max.

My mom. She didn't go back to work for a week, she was so upset."

"I don't care," I replied harshly. What I wanted to say was, *It's not enough. We cried for* months.

But again, I suddenly, vividly, remembered Dr. Drose staggering into the hospital waiting room to deliver the news. How devastated she'd looked, hands shaking and bags under her eyes. How when she told Mom, they'd just hugged and hadn't moved for ages. Not until Mom realized I was crying alone on a nearby chair.

It was the worst day of my life. It had never occurred to me that it might have been the worst for Arsenio's mom too.

An announcement came over the loudspeaker, interrupting us. Mr. Hames bellowed, "Attention, attention! Please report to the observation deck. Takeoff in two minutes, kids. If anyone wants off, now's the time!"

Rhett and Tarynn pushed past us. Tarynn paused only long enough to say, "Observation deck. You heard him!"

Once they thundered down the hall, Arsenio wrung the corner of his leather jacket, glancing back at me. To my surprise, his eyes shone. "I'm sorry for what happened to your dad, Max. If you want to be mad at me, that's okay. But I'd like to be friends again. One day." Then he offered a sad smile and turned down the hallway.

Mr. Hames came up behind me. I barely heard him, not until he asked, "Max, is everything okay?" His eyes trailed after the would-be doctor. "Did you talk with Arsenio?"

The hope in his voice made me furious, and suddenly, this

was the last place I wanted to be. I couldn't just stand in the observation deck listening to my classmates chatter, couldn't accept congratulations for my engineering efforts while my body felt this numb. I couldn't just smile and nod and pretend this conversation hadn't happened, even though the memory of that day in the waiting room was tearing me to bits.

I couldn't do it.

"Leave me *alone*," I snarled, and shoved past Mr. Hames. Down the staircase, into the kitchen, down the ladder, straight to the engine room.

Back to what I knew.

And that was where I stayed for the *Calypso*'s inaugural flight.

12

NEW INSTRUMENT, SAME SOUND

didn't want to think about anything. My ears popped as the pressure regulated, as the heat kicked on, as the artificial gravity amped up to compensate for the loss of Azura's constant spinning. And still I sat, curled against the escape pod docking station, watching the soft purple glow of the Starkwil generator, gripping Mr. Hames's decivox.

I ran my fingers along the polished lacquer, ghosted them over the hollow space between the two metal rods. A beautiful sound breathed from the instrument, softer than the wailing in my mind. Tears tracked down my cheeks. This wasn't Dad's decivox; I had no right playing it. But it felt familiar, comforting, to hold this instrument. If I closed my eyes, it was almost like I was back in that tiny storage closet on the recreation level, passing hours in seconds while India hummed along.

Rhett was wrong. The hydrodriver wasn't my security blanket.

I tweaked the dials and plucked invisible strings, listening to the soft humming of the decivox. It was so unfair. Dad had died two years ago, but he was still a ghost over my shoulder, a weight on my heart. I was sick and tired of the pity. Maybe I just didn't *want* to be friends with Arsenio, okay? Who'd want to befriend a kid who always talked about blood and gore, anyway?

But he was right. The years before Dad died felt like another lifetime, one blurry and discarded. India and I used to be into the gross stuff, back when a fart could make us laugh and bodily fluids were fascinating. Arsenio had been airtight back then.

I was so angry after Dad died. Of course that had seeped into our friendship. And India was loyal; if I didn't like Arsenio anymore, *she* didn't like Arsenio anymore. The guy never stood a chance.

Clenching my eyes shut, I twirled my fingers over the decivox, pulling an anguished, melancholy sound from its depths. Dad once told me music was communication, that a truly gifted musician could tell a story from the rise and fall of a rhythm.

Today, I believed it.

I didn't know how much time passed, but eventually someone knocked softly on the metal wall. I startled, almost dropping the instrument, eyes flying open to see Mr. Hames standing at the base of the ladder, well across the room. Against the soft purple glow of the slipstream generator, his awed expression was hard to miss.

"Oh, Max," he breathed. "That's absolutely incredible."

"What do you want?" I sniffed, rubbing my eyes to hide the last remaining evidence of tears.

Mr. Hames shifted, stepping away from the ladder. "I was worried. India too. She thought maybe you got left behind. She wanted to check, but she's the navigator, so Tarynn wouldn't let her leave the flight deck."

I imagined that fight. Bossy Tarynn squaring off against a stubborn India. Normally, I'd laugh, but I didn't feel like it now. Instead, I set the decivox on the ground and replied, crossly, "Well, I'm here and I'm fine."

"If you want to talk—"

Oh *stars*.

"I don't," I forced through gritted teeth. He looked disappointed, but I kept talking, my voice growing more forceful. "I don't want to talk. If I wanted that, I'd find someone and *talk*, but instead I'm down here playing your decivox, so clearly I don't!"

He considered me for a moment, and I half expected him to scowl, to scold. Mom would have been all over that, shooting me The Look while simultaneously apologizing for my outburst. I'd heard it before: *he's upset, he lost his father, he doesn't mean it.*

But I did mean it. I glared, daring him to say anything.

Of course, he didn't. Nothing about Mr. Hames was normal. In direct opposition to my dark tone, he took a bright, happy one. "Okay. No problem, Max. You can stay down here as long as you'd like. But we're almost to the asteroid belt, so I thought maybe—"

"What?" I interrupted.

He blinked. "Ah, we're almost to the asteroid belt." To prove his point, he nodded to the tiny windows lining the bulkhead walls. I squinted, but the dark shapes drifting before a bright abundance of stars were hard to miss.

"But the asteroid belt is two hours from Azura." I'd lost track of time, sure, but I hadn't been playing that long. No way. And then my eyes settled on the Starkwil generator, and appreciation overtook my irritation. "Wow. This thing *is* fast."

Mr. Hames shrugged, cheeks tinged with pride. "Best in the galaxy—"

A loud wailing cut him off. For a moment, it sounded like someone crying . . . but the tone wasn't sad. I shoved to my feet, and Mr. Hames froze. His voice was distant as he whispered, "It can't be."

We both went silent, trying to identify the source; it seemed to be coming from the ship's loudspeakers. Like an eerie melody from the depths of space.

But that wasn't right. Sound couldn't travel in a vacuum.

Heh. Maybe those cannibalistic space sirens were real after all. Despite my amusement, some scared-little-kid part of my brain whispered, *Don't joke about that.* Instead, I tried the logical route. "Maybe someone hacked us?"

There. That made perfect sense. Maybe one of Azura's miners, playing a prank on the tourist. They probably thought this was funny.

But Mr. Hames looked incredulous. "This—it's not music, Max."

I listened harder, straining to decipher the sound. And then it clicked. He was right. Although the sound was almost like a decivox—that smooth transition of high and low notes, warbling with vibrato—this was clearly organic. And we'd heard something similar in Mrs. Smith's class, during her lectures on poaching—the topic we'd been exploring right before Mr. Hames took control of our class.

It *sounded* like a whale.

"No way," I said.

"After all this time. All these *years*." His eyes flicked to me, to the decivox in my hands, and his eyes widened. "Oh my stars. That's it. Come on!" Mr. Hames ran for the ladder. At the last minute, he spun, jerking a thumb at the instrument. "Bring that. I have a theory."

We scurried upstairs, sprinting to the flight deck. Around us, the melody of the star whales bounced off the metal walls, silencing the entire starship. Even the slipstream generator's rumble was buried underneath it.

Of course, just as we reached the second ladder, a loud argument in the observation deck stopped us short.

"It's right there," Nashira was saying, exasperated. She jabbed a finger at the plastiglass windows, her green leaf earrings swaying as she pointed into space. "Look! How are you missing it?"

"This isn't funny, Nash," Tarynn snapped. "Bad enough the speakers are on the fritz. I don't need hallucinating crew members too!"

Arsenio squinted at the windows, at what was apparently beyond them. Beside him, Rhett scowled. "I don't see anything."

Nashira huffed. "Then you're blind. They're *right there*."

Mr. Hames's breath caught, but before he could move for the observation deck, India's head poked through the circular opening of the ladder. She must have been lying on the floor of the flight deck to get that angle.

"*Max!* Hurry up, you have to see this!"

I wasted no time scaling the ladder, still clutching the decivox. Mr. Hames was close behind, and India scooched out of the way, taking my arm to pull me upright. In front of a massive control panel, Louisa was typing furiously, eyes flicking to the wide window that circled the bullet-like curve of the room. There were two empty chairs—one perched in front of a tiny holographic map of the Fifth Star System, and one opposite it beside a screen broadcasting communication relays beyond the ship.

Mr. Hames reached the top rung of the ladder. "Max, ah, if you don't mind?"

I was blocking him. I pressed against the back wall, behind where the captain's chair should be. But it was just empty space, as if Mr. Hames had decided it wasn't necessary and had it removed. The result was an inviting area for people to mingle, which was probably his intent.

"Max. Max, look!" India towed me to Nashira's chair, pointing to the window beyond him.

And I saw it. A star whale.

I mean, really, it was impossible to miss. It was *massive*, bigger than the asteroids Azurans spent a century mining. The creature pushed them aside like annoying debris, shifting its body like a slow-moving eel. The shape was similar to a whale, certainly, with two massive fins below its oblong torso—*just like the fin Flandius Scoot recovered*, I thought dimly—and a crescent moon of a tail.

That was where the similarities stopped.

I gaped at two huge . . . they could only be described as

sails: big, transparent triangles that stretched like a cape over the star whale's back, glimmering gold in the distant light of a million stars. They rippled fluidly, like fabric through water, and the harder I squinted at them, the more they faded from view. Huge divots on the star whale's nose seemed to glow green, and two long, um, *whiskers*—although they looked closer to stalks of wheat—kept brushing against where its blowhole should be.

But it was the creature's eyes that stole my breath. They glimmered black as the space around us, staring right at me through the windows. When it had my attention, it sang again, louder. Almost . . . inquisitive. Goose bumps pebbled my arms, and I staggered back against India.

"*Stars.*" My throat seized with emotion. If this was what Dad had seen, no *wonder* he'd left Azura.

How could I ever be happy with our tiny space station after this?

"It's beautiful," Louisa whispered.

But that's when Mr. Hames said, "Wait, where is it?" and the breathless awe of the flight deck shattered.

I ripped my gaze from the amazing creature to stare at our substitute teacher, at the man who'd whisked us to the asteroid belt for this very reason. The man who was now squinting through the plastiglass windows, staring *right at the whale,* with confusion and disappointment all over his features.

He could hear the star whale, but—he couldn't see it.

13

THE MUSIC OF SPACE

gripped the decivox to my chest. "It's there, just outside. It's looking right at us."

Mr. Hames pressed closer to the window, desperation evident in the way his teeth clenched, the way his hands pulled at his hair. The whale seemed to move a lot slower than we did, but it shifted position to examine our teacher. Another few feet, and it'd bump right into the *Calypso*.

But realization never crossed Mr. Hames's face.

"You can't see it." It wasn't a question. Once again, my eyes drew to the whale, focusing on the shimmering cape-like sails. They shifted in and out of focus, bright gold one moment and completely see-through the next. It was the oddest thing.

The whale fell silent, almost like it had noticed our disappointment. The soft rumble of the starship's generator seemed so quiet in the wake of such a powerful song.

India frowned. "Maybe it's like those frogs? A defense mechanism." When I raised an eyebrow, she shrugged. "You know. They're in the botanarium." She looked to Louisa for backup, since her mom worked there.

Louisa blushed under the attention, but nodded. "They're, ah, covered in mucus. It helps them absorb oxygen and keeps their skin moist. I think." The last two words were barely a whisper, like she wasn't confident of that.

"And some secrete poison, right?" India grinned.

"Um . . . you should ask Nashira," she said. "She's the one who really likes the botanarium."

India nudged me. "Well, the point stands. A defense mechanism. I bet that's what this is. Maybe the whale is covered in mucus to preserve oxygen in space. And maybe that mucus also hides it from some people's view." The last part of her sentence was inquisitive, and she glanced at Mr. Hames.

He was still gazing out the window, squinting, utterly devastated now. "I—I don't understand. We just *heard* it. And two decades ago, I saw one. What change—" He fell silent, staring at his hands in horror. "Two decades. Age. Oh stars. What if adults can't see them?"

The shattered statement lingered in the air. If that was true, he'd never see them again . . . and considering he'd dedicated his life to the task, considering its majesty now, I understood his grief.

The permanence of never getting to see something you loved again. Well. I could relate.

It wrenched my heart, and I desperately racked my brain for something to disprove the theory. And that's when I remembered our classmates' argument downstairs. I opened my mouth to bring it up when Tarynn poked her head into the flight deck.

"Mr. Hames, Nashira keeps saying the star whale's outside. Tell her to cut it out. Tell her that sound was just the loudspeakers malfunctioning."

"It was not," Nashira called from below, indignant.

There. Theory disproved.

Mr. Hames realized it too, because he spun on Tarynn, eyes widening. Quick as a whip, he surged for the ladder, sliding down the rungs the second she cleared the landing area. The rest of us followed until the entirety of our class was crammed into the observation deck. Nashira stood by the windows, looking indignant, while Tarynn and Rhett perched near the couches, wearing matching expressions of irritation. Arsenio was on the opposite side of the room, rubbing his arm as his eyes grazed the windows. It didn't seem like he could see them either.

India plopped onto the opposite couch, eyes flicking to the star whale beyond the plastiglass. It moved lower, sinking from the flight deck windows to these ones, and an echoing click—like a pulse of sonar—rang through the intercom.

India grinned. She clearly loved that our two most annoying classmates couldn't see it, and she could. "Come on, guys. Did that *really* sound like a malfunctioning loudspeaker?"

"Yes," Rhett growled.

I glanced at the decivox, then at Mr. Hames. "It's trying to talk to us. That's why you wanted me to bring this."

"Brilliant," Nashira exclaimed, capturing our attention. "Microptera communicate like this too. Not body language, but song. *Music.*"

"I've never heard Echo do anything but screech," India said drily.

Nashira stuck out her tongue. "Well, that's their symphony. Don't judge."

Mr. Hames ignored them, striding past me to peer out the

window. "Music. You're right, Max. When I heard you play, it reminded me of the whales back when I was a child. So I thought, maybe—"

In response, I tucked the decivox under my arm, twirling my fingers around the hollow belly of the instrument. Now that I was comparing the sound, it *was* remarkably similar to the whale's. The thought filled me with satisfaction, like another piece of the puzzle sliding into place.

I bet that was why Dad learned this instrument in the first place. Who wouldn't want to communicate with star whales? I played a quick melody, twisting the top dial slowly so the thin vibrato rose in pitch until it was almost like a musical question.

A test.

The resulting silence was deafening. After a moment, India huffed. "Some invisible creatures just can't appreciate good music."

But then the whale replied, a happy trill of fast beats. It didn't take a musician to comprehend its mirth. I stared into its black, glimmering eyes, and the certainty of our exchange settled into my bones.

A smile spread across my face.

Nashira rubbed the leaves of her earrings, jaw dropping. "Wow."

Mr. Hames put a hand on the window, forlornly. "So we can talk to it. Some of us just can't *see* it." He spun back to us, forcing a smile. "I think you're right, India. All this time, and no whaler ever considered that *stella cetacea* might be hiding in plain sight."

His eyes slid to the three kids who couldn't see it: Tarynn, Rhett, and Arsenio. "So . . . what do we have in common?"

"You're all sticks in the mud," India drawled. "Except you, Mr. Hames. You're just old."

"Thanks," he said.

Tarynn sniffed. "I'm not a stick in the mud. I'm *mature*, unlike you."

"Childish and proud of it," India shot back.

My hand brushed against my leather jacket's pocket, against the smoke bomb she'd tucked in there earlier this week, and I laughed. Truer words were never spoken.

"No, wait," Mr. Hames exclaimed. "You're absolutely right. Maturity. Tarynn and Arsenio are trying to be like their parents. And Rhett, based on what you've told me, you never had a choice. Your parents expect an adult attitude, no matter your age."

Rhett shifted, shooting me a glare when I squinted at him. "They want me to succeed. Which is more than *you* can say, Belmont." He sniffed, smoothing his impeccable outfit. It was almost a nervous tick, checking the state of his clothes. I'd never noticed before.

Kind of made me wonder what his life was like outside of school.

Mr. Hames shifted his gaze to the window. "These whales . . . They're amazing. *Wondrous.* And by normal standards, they shouldn't exist. Maybe that's their defense mechanism. They hide from people who lack the hope and wonder you kids carry so easily. They hide from anyone who isn't imaginative enough to appreciate them."

The whale trilled again, as if in agreement. It was a bright, happy sound, but it seemed to make Mr. Hames sadder. He drew a deep, shaking breath and turned to Tarynn.

"Okay, Madam First Officer. I have an important question for you." When she pulled back her shoulders, puffing her chest, he laughed. For a moment, the crushing sadness at missing the star whales vanished, and our bright, weird teacher was back. "What was your favorite game as a kid?"

"Um . . ." Tarynn glanced at us, cheeks darkening. She turned her nose up. "I didn't play games."

Mr. Hames tilted his head. "You know what I liked? Spot the Star. My friends and I would stare into the cosmos and craft all kinds of exciting stories about the stars we saw. What orbited them? Was there life? What did it look like? We'd play for hours. Did you have anything like that?"

A long moment stretched, and finally Tarynn hung her head in defeat. Her words were mumbled, but in the quiet of the room, we all heard. "I-I used to like smugglers-and-security."

Wow. I'd forgotten India and Tarynn and I used to play that game together. We were *little* back then, maybe four or five, but it was fun. Then she got bossy and rude, and we started playing without her.

From the way she glowered at us now, she clearly hadn't forgiven us for that.

Oops.

"Okay, great," Mr. Hames said encouragingly. "Remember the hours of fun you had playing that? Try to remember the possibility, all the creativity, how easily those ideas came to you."

Outside the windows, the whale shifted its body away from us. Like we were boring, like it had better things, whale things, to do. It paused at a weird-looking asteroid: the shiny kind that indicated anemonium was prevalent, the kind our miners *loved* to see, the kind that used to be all over the asteroid belt before Azura and space stations like it broke those asteroids into tinier and tinier chunks. The whale then twisted around it, as if that asteroid was fire and it didn't want to get burned.

Weird.

I considered playing a few notes on my decivox, just to see if I could regain its attention, but I didn't want to interrupt Mr. Hames's attempt to help Tarynn. Besides, the whale moved so slowly, we still had plenty of time.

Tarynn closed her eyes, really trying what Mr. Hames suggested. It was stupid and insane, but that was a running theme on the *Calypso*. Even India kept quiet. I think we all wanted our classmates to see the beauty of the star whale before it left. It didn't seem fair that we were part of the same crew, yet having different experiences.

Then, several feet from Tarynn, Arsenio gasped. "W-wait a minute. That's been there the whole time?"

Rhett inhaled sharply a moment after that. He didn't shout or cheer. Instead, he glanced at Tarynn, as if seeing the star whale was a direct betrayal to her.

And based on her frustrated scowl, maybe it was. "Why can't I see it, Mr. Hames? I want to see the whale too!"

"It's leaving," Nashira said. "Max, can't you bring it back?"

I cranked up the volume and played a few notes, slipping

some of our desperation into the tune. But the star whale kept swimming away, offering only a few beats of song in response. I could imagine it saying, *"This was fun, but I have to go."*

I lowered the instrument. "Sorry. I think it got bored."

"I mean, it's probably like looking at fish in a tank," India mused. "Fun for a while, but not somewhere to waste an afternoon. You know?"

Rhett stepped to Tarynn's side, taking her hand. He pointed their clasped fingers at the star whale. "It's huge, Rynn. Close your eyes and imagine it. It has these golden sails, bigger than the *Calypso*."

Behind them, Louisa added, quietly, "And long, thin whiskers. Like—like tassels on a graduation cap."

Arsenio beamed. "And its eyes are—"

"Black as ink," Tarynn said, eyes widening as she focused on the star whale for the first time.

Rhett released her hand, grinning. "Right." Even slowly retreating, the creature was breathtaking, exquisite. Its tail waved as if saying goodbye, and the golden capes on its back flared out like a boat's sails. It started picking up speed, close to breaking through the asteroid belt into open space now. India laughed, then Tarynn, and soon the entire class was giggling, swept into the adventure of a lifetime.

Well, the entire class, except for Mr. Hames.

He'd turned from the windows, and his expression made my stomach twist. Been a while since I'd literally seen a heart break. Two years, actually . . . not since the day Mom and Dr. Drose embraced and cried, and I realized Dad wasn't coming home, ever.

Now I found that same anguish in our teacher. His eyes shone, and he stared at the ceiling as if the dim lights would hide his despair. What must it be like, to search for something your entire life, only to realize you could never see it? How close had he come to a star whale during his decades of travel? How many times had it glided past, magnificent and bold, to the complete oblivion of the *Calypso*'s crew? Or the *Enrapture*'s?

He was annoying and weird and pried too much, but I felt bad for him. He'd given me the rare experience of fixing a Starkwil generator, something my dad had only dreamed about. He'd lent me a decivox just because he knew I enjoyed playing one. And if today was any indication, I wasn't the only kid in class he'd helped.

And now he needed us. I nudged India's shoulder and mouthed, "Follow my lead," then crept to Mr. Hames's side. He didn't notice us, not until I took one hand. A moment later, without question, India took the other.

"What?" Mr. Hames said, voice wobbling.

I put a finger to my lips and turned him back to the window. He squinted at the asteroid belt. The whale may be leaving, but its golden sails still shimmered, its massive tail still defined.

There was still time.

"You're not giving yourself enough credit, Mr. Hames. Go with me here," I said. Beside us, the rest of the class watched curiously. At India's beckoning, Nashira and Louisa took our free hands, and Rhett and Tarynn took theirs, then Arsenio, until everyone was linked in one long chain against the plastiglass.

Mr. Hames's eyes watered, but he didn't interrupt me as I

said, "I think you've spent too long with boring adults. Thinking about money, worrying about deadlines, taking this job even if you didn't want to, just because it's the grown-up thing to do."

"Well, I can't feed myself without digits—" he began, but I squeezed his hand, cutting him off.

India stepped in, seamlessly picking up my train of thought. "That's a problem for later. When you're the captain of the *Calypso*, when we're your crew, you're not a boring adult. You're the cool substitute teacher who raves about trees the size of planets and being mermaids. You're the traveler who collects souvenirs from every place you visit, even when they're dangerous . . . and possibly fatal. Even when you definitely don't have room for them."

He chuckled weakly. "I think you kids have too much faith in me."

"*I* think you don't have enough faith in yourself," Tarynn said, and somehow she made even that sound bossy.

Mr. Hames carefully extracted his hand from mine, scrubbing his face. "Look, I'm not—trying to be difficult. It's just that I've spent so many hours staring out the windows, scouring space for a hint I'm not wasting my time. And all that experience isn't even helping me here." He hung his head.

The whale was going to be gone soon, and our teacher was sinking into despair.

So I kicked his shin.

"Ow!" he yelped, hopping a bit. "Max, that was really rude!"

"Don't scold me like I'm a kid. That's why you're not seeing the whale." I shoved the decivox at him. "This is *your* instrument.

Your ship. Your *idea* to come out here at all. It's pretty lame you're giving up before you even try."

Mr. Hames's eyes flashed. "I'm not giving up—"

"Seems like you are," India drawled. Her voice climbed in pitch, even though Mr. Hames's tone was decidedly lower than hers. "'All that experience isn't helping me here.' Life's not about experience. Life's about possibility."

Tarynn chimed in. "And frankly, Mr. Hames, I'm *way* more mature than you. So if I can see it, you can."

I took his hand again, pointing him back toward the window. "It's almost gone, but you deserve to see it too. Come on. How did you feel when you first saw the whale, years ago?"

Mr. Hames looked close to breaking, but he reluctantly returned his gaze to the windows. It was obvious he still didn't see it, based on his crestfallen expression. But he dutifully muttered, "Um, I felt so happy. It was inspiring. I was—well, we were on a refugee ship after the war on Hysteria. My family left *everything* behind." Tears welled in his eyes, and he scrubbed his nose against his shoulder. "It was a real low point for us. But when it swam past the windows, it was like giving me new purpose. I wasn't scared anymore."

Oh. Wow. India and I exchanged horrified looks. That—that was really devastating. I suddenly felt really terrible for yelling at him last week, for kicking his shin just a few minutes ago.

But I could relate to the whales breathing new purpose into life. This one was almost gone; just the outline and the shimmer of its gold cape remained. I pointed to where it was and said, desperately, "Feel those emotions again. Imagine that moment."

Mr. Hames went silent, staring through the plastiglass.

And then—

—then he laughed.

"T-there it is. Stars, it's been *so long*." He squeezed my hand so hard it hurt, but I didn't have the heart to pull away. Tears streamed down his cheeks, which was awkward even though they were happy tears, not sad ones. "*Stella cetacea*. I can't believe we found it! And that instrument—all this time, the decivox was the key to calling it over."

Cautiously, he released my hands. I waited, but his wonder never vanished. Even without a physical connection to us, he could still see it.

"Amazing." He leaned his forehead against the plastiglass, beaming. "Thank you, guys. Stars, this is the happiest day of my life."

I shoved my hands into my pockets, trying to look bored instead of stupidly pleased. "Sure. Whatever."

But it was probably the happiest day of mine too.

14

THE PROBLEM WITH MESSAGING

We got away with it. Somehow, some way, the entire twelfth-year class of Azura took an unsanctioned trip to the asteroid belt, and *no one noticed*.

It was kind of remarkable. When Mr. Hames parked his starship, when the staircase hissed open and the pressurization equalized and our ears popped as we stepped off the *Calypso*, I think everyone expected a welcoming party. At the very least, my mom should have been there, red with anger, waiting to drag me back to safety.

But Louisa's hack had worked, and Nashira's radio recordings had been flawless, and when our class went their separate ways, it was with wide grins and the knowledge of a secret so big, it'd be the gossip of the century.

And yet, for once, none of us would dare reveal it. There was no social standing greater than the knowledge that we shared something special, something magical. We were a crew now, in this together.

So when Mr. Hames opened the loading bay for the *Calypso* and said, "I'm sure I don't have to remind you, but this has to stay with the ship," we were already nodding in agreement. Especially when he added, "If anyone finds out, our excursions are done."

So there'd be more. Already, India and I exchanged excited glances. We'd only just left the star whale, but I couldn't wait to get back to the asteroid belt, play the decivox again, and talk to a creature bigger than most starships.

The thrill of the secret thumped my heart.

But India was staring at our class president. "Tarynn." Her voice held warning.

The whole class turned to face her, desperation etched in all of our expressions.

She glanced between us, huffed, and snapped, "I wasn't going to say anything! I'm a professional. You should be looking at Nashira. She's the gossiper here."

"Communications expert, thank you." Nashira sniffed. "And please. The whale might be more interesting than Echo. I have to get back out there."

Mr. Hames shot us a pleading look. "Guys. I'm counting on you. Promise?"

"We won't tell," I reassured him.

"Promise," India replied, without a hint of a joke.

The other kids voiced their agreement, and we all gathered together to tap elbows—the sign of friendship and agreement. After a moment, Mr. Hames joined, smiling. "Thanks, kids. See you all next week."

Now we were a crew, in this together. Waving goodbye to Mr. Hames, we filed off his ship, chatting pointedly about everything but the star whale.

Of course, this wasn't the only secret I was keeping, so when the rest of the class crammed into a central elevator, I held back. India glanced at me, raising an eyebrow, but I waved her on with a clarifying excuse: "Mr. Keller."

She huffed. "You have a decivox now, Max. Why do you need to work for him anymore?"

What? I crossed my arms, not bothering to hide the hurt in my voice. "It was never about the decivox."

She heard what I didn't say. That Mr. Hames's decivox couldn't replace my dad's, even if his worked and mine didn't. It wasn't the same. Her cheeks colored, and she sighed. "Okay. Sorry. We'll see you tomorrow."

To my surprise, a few of our classmates turned and yelled, "Bye, Max!" and "See you, man!"

We hadn't had this kind of camaraderie in years.

I waved, and a pang of loneliness hit as India turned to the group, away from me. She was laughing when the elevator doors closed, and then I was alone, bouncing in the questionable gravity as another lift arrived. Swallowing my guilt, I stepped inside, pressing the button not for Mr. Keller's shop but for the civil center. The library was calling my name.

As I settled into a chair near Mr. Krad's desk, powering on the behemoth of a computer, I reminded myself that I'd *chosen* this. India and my classmates would always be there, but it wasn't every day I could chat with my dad's best friend.

I opened our messages, my heart racing. It took just a minute to type a quick hello, and then I glanced at the clock, counting down the seconds. He always replied fast, within ten minutes or so. I wouldn't have to wait long.

Except today, fifteen minutes crept by.

Twenty.

Thirty.

Maybe he was busy. Adults usually had things to do. Even when Mom was home, if work had an emergency, she'd dive into her holopad to help. Dad used to drop pieces of the mineships on our kitchen table after dinner, and I'd do my homework to the quiet whirring of his hydrodriver.

I couldn't fault Kane for having a job. But that didn't stop the disappointment curdling in the pit of my stomach. I'd chosen to come to the library, made an excuse and everything, instead of hanging with my friends after the most airtight experience ever. Even if I left the library now, it was too late to pretend Mr. Keller didn't need me today. India was already suspicious; she'd see right through that lie.

Which meant, if Kane didn't reply, I'd have to go home. And sit alone in our apartment until Mom got home and cooked dinner. It was the worst feeling, staring at a space once vibrant and alive, knowing my dad would never stroll through the hallways, complain about work, ruffle my hair, and sit on the floor to keep me company.

No, going home was my last resort. At least until Mom finished work.

Plus, if Mom came home to find me already there waiting, she'd know something was up. She'd ask all kinds of prying questions. And thanks to her uncanny ability to tell when I was lying, she'd find out about our trip to the asteroid belt, and me fixing the slipstream generator, and the star whales, and I'd be grounded forever—

The computer pinged, and a response to my message appeared.

Kane!

Hey there, kid. Sorry. With the deadline coming up, we're in fight mode over here. No space stone left unturned, right? I hate to say it, because I've enjoyed our chats, but I just don't have time to talk right now. I'm sure you'll have enough fun chatting with Milo instead!

What? Panic had goose bumps pricking my arms, and my heart thumped heavily. No. No no no. This wasn't fair! Kane was the last real connection I had with my dad. If he vanished, I was back to life before this week.

Back to knowing nothing at all.

Well, not nothing. Because today we'd learned something no whaler in three centuries could figure out. Something Kane would undoubtedly find very interesting. Maybe if I told him what we'd seen, he'd find a bit more time for me.

But my hands stilled over the holographic keyboard. Mr. Hames had been clear. *"This stays with the ship."* I knew what my class would say, what they'd think. *Tattletale. Snitch.* But Kane didn't know anyone on Azura. He'd never even been here. It couldn't hurt, right?

Guilt still tightened my chest, though. Desperate, I skimmed through the messages we'd exchanged in the last few days. Every one of them mentioned the star whales in some capacity. It had been a huge part of Dad's life back then, and it was still a huge part of Kane's.

He'd been so nice. He'd told me everything about Dad, answered all my questions. It shouldn't matter what my classmates thought of this—technically, this secret belonged to me, my dad, Kane, and Mr. Hames. They were just the lucky kids who were pulled along for the ride, but their passing interest couldn't hold more weight than mine. And if Kane wanted to see a star whale as badly as Mr. Hames, who was I to refuse?

I drafted a message.

I didn't tell him everything, obviously. The whole "visible through childlike wonder" thing was an unproven theory at best, and I didn't want to lose face by mentioning something Kane might have already disproved. But he couldn't argue we'd seen one.

I rewrote the message six times, praying it didn't sound desperate. Praying he'd think it was interesting enough to discuss, and not just some unverified sighting like those cruise ship passengers. I added enough chatter to keep a conversation going, then ended with:

Mr. Hames took us to the asteroid belt today, and we saw a star whale. It came right up to our ship! You should have been there.

Fingers trembling, I sent it.

His reply was instantaneous.

A star whale? Really? Way out in your asteroid belt?

Now we were getting somewhere. Satisfaction swelled, and I couldn't resist boasting.

Yeah! Dad saw them at least twice out here. I think they like the cover. Better to hide between the asteroids, maybe? But it was awesome!

I thought that would open a dialogue, but Kane's next message didn't leave much room for discussion.

Amazing!

That was it. Just one word. It felt like a punch in the gut. Two days ago, he'd been writing essays about Dad and life on the *Enrapture*, and now I barely pulled one word from him. My heart sank, and I waited to see if he'd add anything else.

Fifteen minutes.

Twenty.

Thirty.

Finally, Mr. Krad tapped my shoulder, squinting past his thick glasses. "Library's closin', kid. Get on home." For someone who didn't see very well, he stared pretty hard as I powered down the machine and trudged for the door.

While he locked the door behind me, I tried not to feel like I'd messed up big time.

15

FAUX-FAMILY DINNER

I staggered through the housing level, numb. This was the biggest level of Azura, taller than the biggest hangar and wider than the botanarium. It was the only multistory level we had too; miniature elevators connected five huge floors of two hundred apartments each, which overlooked a shared hallway brimming with trees and star-side views. Unlike the other areas, where I could sometimes find peace, this level was always bustling. I shared the elevator with three others, but I didn't drag my gaze off the ground to see who.

Of course, outside apartment 542, I ran into the person I *least* wanted to see.

"Mr. Hames?" I demanded.

He spun, tugging at his collar, cheeks almost as red as his hair. In his hands was a tiny wrapped box with a big purple bow, and he'd swapped his leather jacket out for a tweed replacement. It looked comically outdated.

But even staring at him now, my guilt compounded into full-on nausea. He'd asked me to stay quiet, and I'd just blurted our secret to Kane. Maybe Kane really didn't care. Maybe he was following some other lead across the galaxy. But if anyone found out . . . if Mr. Hames found out . . . I'd be done for.

Snitch. Tattletale.

Liar.

Mr. Hames beamed. "Ah, Max! Hello! Sorry for the confusion, but I was—"

"Invited for dinner," Mom finished. I hadn't even seen her open the door. "Come in, Milo, come in. We're happy to have you."

"We are?" I blurted before I could stop myself.

Mom shot me The Look. "Yes. Of course we are."

Mr. Hames offered her the tiny box. "It's really kind of you to invite me here. I don't know many people on Azura, so this is lovely. H-here! It's Uphronian chocolate. Smoothest in the galaxy, or so they say!"

Oh, he was good. Mom was a sucker for chocolate. She held up her hands, but I saw the gleam in her eyes as she said, "Oh, that's really too much. It's just dinner. We wouldn't want to take—"

"Nonsense," he interrupted, flashing a gracious smile. "Really, Camille. I appreciate this. Eating alone gets tiring after the first few months."

What was he doing? Didn't he realize that Mom was like . . . like a cannibalistic siren, except instead of blood, she could smell *deceit* from a planet away? All she'd have to do was listen to me stutter, and she'd know we had a secret. Forget Kane. If we made it through dinner without her discovering the star whales, it'd be a miracle.

"Well, then. How can I refuse?" Mom said, and took the box with a grin. I followed Mr. Hames inside, kicking off my shoes as she set the chocolate—almost reverently—on the kitchen counter. She'd been cooking for a while already; the hearty smell of vegetable stew filled the house. She motioned for Mr. Hames to take a seat at our table, then opened the crisper. "Would you like something to drink?"

I tuned out their pleasantries, brainstorming ideas to get out of this. Maybe I could swipe Mom's holopad, shoot India an SOS. But she'd have to be near a holopad herself, and since she and her mom attended yoga in the recreation level most nights before dinner, chances of that were slim.

Maybe I could fake a stomachache. If I wasn't feeling well, Mr. Hames would have to leave. But would that be more or *less* suspicious than just sitting down to eat? Hard to tell with Mom.

I glanced at my bedroom, two doors down the apartment's hallway. I still had India's smoke bomb. Maybe I could fake some kind of emergency. Something to evacuate the—

"Max. Stop scheming and come sit down," Mom said in her no-nonsense tone.

Stars, she saw everything. I forced a laugh, one of those "oh, Mom, you're going crazy" type chuckles, but trudged to the dinner table. This was happening. Dinner with my teacher.

Awkward.

Mr. Hames didn't seem to think so. He took a sip from his water glass, glancing around the apartment with interest. Mom decorated with cool-blue accents and white pillows, and filled the walls with family portraits. Having Mr. Hames staring at our most treasured moments felt like a breach of privacy, even if they were on display. I scowled, but he just said, "You have a beautiful home, Camille. Are all the apartments in Azura this roomy?"

"There are a few sizes, some smaller, some bigger," she replied, collecting the bowls in front of us and filling them with stew. Mr. Hames jumped up to help, but she waved him off. "Oh, I've got it. Anyway, space is limited on Azura, so citizens have to apply for housing changes—upgrades and the like."

"Oh, fascinating! I'd imagine on a space station, that type of thing has to be carefully regulated."

"Indeed. Why do you ask? Thinking of sticking around?"

The question was innocent enough, but I didn't miss the way she studied him over the table. Something clicked in my mind. This wasn't some parent-teacher conference at all. For once, I wasn't the subject of scrutiny.

Mr. Hames was.

Somehow, that was even scarier. Sweat trickled down my neck, even as I mumbled thanks and accepted the bowl of stew.

Mr. Hames breezed past Mom's comment, shaking his head. "Oh, no, no. Azura is very nice, but . . . have ship, will travel, right?"

"Well, even travelers need a home base, don't they?"

"I've lived on the *Calypso* most of my adult life. I'm not sure I'd know what to do with something like this." He gestured at our apartment, expression sheepish.

Mom raised one eyebrow. "Then you're not planning to stick around? You told the mayor you'd finish the school year, at least."

Mr. Hames stiffened. *Finally*, he'd figured out what was

happening. His eyes flicked to mine, and I tried to telepathically whisper, *If there's ever a time to lie, now's it!*

"O-oh, yes. Yes, of course! I couldn't leave the kiddos unattended," Mr. Hames said, clearing his throat.

Mom took a seat beside me, across from Mr. Hames, and steepled her fingers. Her sharp gaze seemed to pin him to the table. "Milo. I've got to be honest. The other teachers have complained to Kyrene—ah, the mayor—about the field study program."

Mr. Hames plastered a smooth smile on his face, swallowing a bite of stew. "Well, I was promised two weeks, so we wrapped it up today. Never fear; we'll be back in Classroom 7 before you can blink."

Mom's voice was honey. "And how did it go? Did you learn a lot, Max?"

"The Starkwil generator is amazing," I said, because it was the one honest thing I could think of. Then I shoved a bite of stew into my mouth and made a big show of chewing so she wouldn't ask me anything else.

Her eyes flicked back to Mr. Hames. "The other teachers are concerned that it was a waste of time. According to Natalia, you were supposed to be covering poaching."

"That we did," Mr. Hames replied easily.

I swallowed a snort.

"Really?" Mom blinked.

"Of course. Although I'm a little perturbed the other teachers didn't bring this issue to me directly, instead of gossiping about it behind my back." Mom had the decency to look embarrassed now, but Mr. Hames cleared his throat and moved the conversation forward. "I'm not sure how anyone can think that sitting in a tiny classroom, staring numbly at a VR simulation or holoscreen slideshows, is the best way to learn. Stars, Camille, does that really hold their attention?"

"Well—"

"It doesn't," I muttered, spooning my stew.

Mom frowned.

Mr. Hames ran a hand through his hair. "I'm not trying to cause problems. But where I'm from, kids understand by doing. By *experiencing*. Imagine what they'd miss, sitting in a classroom all day?"

The star whales. We'd have missed the star whales.

Suddenly, gratitude choked me. That had been the most magnificent event of my life, and a more conventional teacher wouldn't have let it happen. We all knew Mr. Hames could get in trouble for taking us off-station. The fact that he'd still done it spoke volumes.

And it made me feel even worse about breaking his trust.

Mom glanced at me, but I didn't dare interrupt again. Her sigh was soft, almost defeated. "It's exciting to see new methods on Azura. But we have a lot of traditionalists here. You're not making friends by breaking the rules."

"Well, maybe it's time for the rules to be challenged," Mr. Hames replied, tilting his head. "This is how innovation begins, Camille. Don't you want it to start with your son?"

She straightened, clearly taken aback. A fond smile spread across her face, and she rubbed at her eyes. "That's how my husband used to talk."

I shoved to my feet.

Dinner with my teacher, sure. Whatever. Let him come into our home, sit at our table, eat our food. Let them discuss Azuran apartments, Azuran lifestyles. Let him and Mom hash out teaching methods while the kid it impacted sat in silence.

But at no point was I okay with bringing *Dad* into this conversation.

Especially not as a comparison to Mr. Hames.

"Max!" Mom exclaimed, but I'd played nice, and now I owed them nothing. Without a word, I stomped into my bedroom and slammed the door.

Silence rang in my wake. Mom spluttered an apology, the same one she always used these days, but Mr. Hames brushed it off. Their voices lowered to the hushed whisper adults used when they were talking about kids—but didn't want said kids eavesdropping. Fine by me. I couldn't care less what they had to say.

Eyes burning, I shuffled to my bed, rumpled from the evening before. I had a few VR simulators stacked on my bedside table, but I didn't feel like playing. Through the wide window, the Kialoa Nebula gleamed pink, purple, blue, gaseous and huge. Under the plastiglass, my desk sat undisturbed, adorned with a few e-book discs, a plant from the botanarium, a solar lamp, and—another holographic photo, one of Dad and Mom and me at the Founding Day celebration three years ago.

Our *last* Founding Day celebration.

My fingers curled around the black display disc, and I collapsed on my mattress, staring at the image. Every detail was familiar. Dad's messy hair, ruffled from a day's work. Mom had been so frustrated when he sprinted through the door minutes before we'd planned to leave, covered in grease and gasping apologies. He changed in record time, but she was still exasperated . . . until he won some silly antique game they'd imported for the celebration and gifted her with a stuffed microptera. The tiny bat-like creature was bright pink and lived in my bed, nestled between my pillows.

I swallowed past the lump in my throat, drowning in the memories of a better time. Stars, I missed Dad so much.

Outside, Mom said, pointedly, "We'll do this again, Milo."

He replied, also too loud, "I'd love that. Thanks for dinner." And the front door opened and shut.

I set the disc on my nightstand, burying my face in my pillows. A few minutes later, Mom knocked on the bedroom door. "Max? Can I come in?"

"Whatever," I said.

The door creaked open, and the bed sagged. I half expected her to start scolding me, but her next words were questioning, careful. "Is everything okay, honey? That was . . . uncharacteristic."

"Well, maybe you should give me a heads-up before inviting my *teacher* over for dinner."

"Max," Mom said. "What's really going on here?"

"Nothing's going on. I just already see Mr. Hames during the day, so I'm not sure why he has to hang around at night too."

"He's lonely. Imagine not having India to laugh with. How would that make you feel?"

Guilt pricked my chest. Probably exactly how Arsenio felt,

faced with an old friend who barely offered more than cold comments these days.

And it was cruelly ironic, because even though we joked and laughed like nothing was wrong, I'd be blind to miss how India had been drifting the last couple of weeks—which was also Mr. Hames's fault. Anything I said now would be snarky and rude, so I clamped my mouth shut and gripped the pillow harder.

Mom sighed. "Honey, is this really about Mr. Hames?"

It was so obvious she wanted to say, *Is this about your father?*

But she didn't, and the unspoken phrase hung like a weight between us. Tears leaked from my eyes, seeping into the soft fabric of the pillow. She couldn't even say Dad's name. This was what he'd been reduced to: a topic neither of us dared to discuss.

A memory, shoved into a box in our minds.

I couldn't take it anymore.

"Why are you hanging out with Arsenio's mom?"

Mom looked taken aback, quirking one delicate eyebrow. "She's one of my oldest friends."

"She *killed* Dad," I whispered into the pillow.

"Max," Mom said, sternly, almost angrily. "Don't you *dare* go around saying that. That's an unkind and insensitive thing to accuse someone of—especially someone who tried so hard to save—" Her voice broke, and she cleared her throat. When I glanced over my shoulder, she was rubbing her eyes.

Crying.

I flinched, feeling like someone had plunged a dagger into my heart. "S-sorry."

Mom pushed to her feet, inhaling shakily. "Sofía is the only reason he lasted as long as he did, Max. Honey, you have to un-derstand she tried—" Mom stopped, drew a few more shattered breaths, then pressed a hand to her heart. "She tried. Some t-things just aren't meant to be."

So I wasn't meant to have a dad?

Tears leaked down my face too, but it hurt more seeing them on Mom's cheeks. I turned back into the pillow, silent.

Eventually, Mom whispered, "I'll bring you some stew later, okay? And, Max, if you ever want to talk, I'm still here."

I'm still here.

I stifled a sob, staying perfectly still until the weight at the foot of my bed lifted, until the door squeaked shut, until I was alone.

16

MR. HAMES, TEACHER EXTRAORDINAIRE

To make matters worse, over the weekend, strange starships began to arrive.

It started with one. A sleek Helion model, pinging Azura for permission to land and "explore." A tourist ship, which of course had Mom springing into action despite our weekend routine of pajamas and ice cream and VR games. I ghosted behind, watching her guide this new ship into Hangar 57. Mayor Zhang arrived, fixing her suit jacket, to greet the newcomer.

An hour later, a second ship arrived.

Then a third. And a fourth.

Soon, Kaito the space traffic controller had a waiting list for hangars and Mayor Zhang had given up welcoming them. The circular corridor on the hangar level bustled with strangers, and from what I gleaned off Mom, they all claimed to be tourists, following a tip of "great views" near Azura.

When the weekend ended and class began, it was with hushed whispers in Classroom 7.

"They're whalers," Arsenio said, rubbing his fingers nervously against his leather jacket. "Right? They're obviously whalers like Mr. Hames."

Our substitute teacher hadn't arrived yet, but that wasn't odd. If we'd learned anything over the last two weeks, it was that he wasn't great at keeping time.

Nashira sniffed, unzipping her backpack to peer at Echo. The tiny creature squeaked, a high-pitched sound that made the rest of us flinch. She just beamed at it, petting its massive ears with one finger. "Whoever they are, Uncle Amir said they're everywhere, asking all kinds of questions. Our parents got really paranoid; Mom want us to come straight home after school."

That made the rest of us go quiet, exchanging glances. Azura was safe. Everyone knew everyone. If Nashira's uncle—the *chief of police*—didn't think the twins should be wandering now that strangers had spread like a virus, was it dangerous for us too?

Louisa tapped something into her holopad, gnawing on her lower lip. "I-I got footage of some of their hangars. Some of the whalers are stringing surveillance equipment in the corridor. Like they're, um, monitoring the competition."

"Competition for *what*?" India exclaimed, gripping the corners of her desk. "I'm so confused."

"It's because of the deadline," I said quietly.

Yet again, the room went silent as everyone swiveled their heads toward me. Tarynn stomped right up to my desk, glaring. "What deadline, Max?"

I hadn't told them about it. There hadn't been a need. Regardless of why Mr. Hames wanted to go into space, our class craved the adventure, so expanding on his motivations wouldn't have changed their minds.

But now everyone was staring, and Tarynn rapped her knuckles on my desk, so I replied, "There's a government grant. A million digits to whoever finds 'undeniable proof' of a star whale's existence."

"Why would they care?" Rhett raised an eyebrow.

Nashira rolled her eyes. "Think about it, Rhett. Those creatures must play some role in their ecosystem. I bet they benefit the environment in ways we can't fathom."

I thought back to how the whale interacted with the asteroid belt, how it skated around one of the few silvery asteroids still left after the mining boom. Odd that it'd push the other ones aside like they were water but swim around an asteroid brimming with anemonium, the material responsible for Azura's creation in the first place.

Wonder if anyone else noticed that.

"Hang on. We found a star whale," Tarynn exclaimed, indignant. "We should be able to claim that money for Azura."

I rolled my eyes. "Hundreds of people have seen it, but it's not enough. I think the government wants the actual whale."

"What, like, capturing it?" India asked, narrowing her eyes at me. "That's not fair. It didn't hurt anyone. Why should it have to live in a cage somewhere?"

"And where would they find a cage big enough?" Nashira wondered, tugging her earring so hard one of the green leaves ripped.

Arsenio swallowed, minimizing the golden game perpetually

open in the classroom. "It's not . . . *that* crazy. Think of all the progress we could make studying a creature like that. One whale's existence for the betterment of humanity doesn't seem like a bad trade." The looks he received were pure venom, but although he wavered, he didn't back down. "C-come on, guys. How do you think we develop vaccines or combat diseases? It's all animal research. And something like this is . . . is revolutionary."

India spun on him, and he hunched in his desk. Her voice was sharp as a knife. "You know what we don't do, Arsenio? Capture magnificent, amazing creatures that might be *very* endangered."

"*Or* take one out of its environment when we don't know how it even *affects* the asteroid belt. What if it's—blocking radiation from reaching us, or something?" Nashira huffed. "Ecosystems are fragile things, Arsenio."

He hung his head, silent now.

But India had to throw in one final jab. "Honestly, with that attitude, I'm shocked you saw the star whale at all."

Arsenio looked close to tears. He glanced at me, then sank into his seat. I flinched at the defeat in his eyes—like he hoped, in passing, that I might stand up for him . . . until he remembered we weren't friends anymore.

My fault. *My fault.* I inhaled shakily, then made a decision. I took India's arm and whispered, "Too far," before towing her back to her seat. And even though she gaped like *I* was wrong, I didn't regret it.

Because his argument made sense, and it was yet another reason why I bet Dad was okay with the whalers of the *Enrapture*. Already, I was crafting a story in my head to fit this narrative.

Maybe Dad wanted to capture a star whale for research, not for digits. *For the betterment of humanity,* like Arsenio said.

But without talking to Kane, I'd never know. And he hadn't messaged me in days.

And now whalers were on Azura because I'd spilled our secret.

I ignored Arsenio's grateful look, taking my own seat beside India. He wouldn't be grateful for long. None of them would—not once they discovered what I'd done. Anxiety had my heart thumping against my chest, my mind buzzing like a swarm of bees.

"I don't understand," Tarynn said into the silence. A rare admission, for her. "If these strangers really are whalers, how did they know we found one?"

Rhett sniffed, smoothing his gray vest. "It's too big a coincidence. Someone must have snitched."

Well, that didn't take long. I sank into my seat, cursing myself. I'd told a prominent whaler about finding the creature of his fantasies, then just expected him to *not* follow up.

Stupid. *Stupid.*

Everyone glared, accusations tipping their tongues, but before they could start pointing fingers, Mr. Hames burst into the classroom. Although he was wearing our uniform, everything about him was more disheveled than usual, from his red hair in matted knots to the deep bags under his eyes to the frantic way he fumbled with at least sixteen display discs.

We took our seats as he tossed the display discs on his desk, moving the tiny metal rectangles aside to find the right one. "Kids! Thank the stars you're all here. We don't have time to waste!" Distracted, he pressed a button to display the image, then enlarged it with a wave of his hand.

"Are they whalers, Mr. Hames?" Tarynn demanded.

He barely spared her a glance. "Of *course* they're whalers. They must have found out about our excursion somehow. Haven't figured that out yet. Working on it. Maybe someone told them, but none of you know any whalers, and I assume you weren't idiotic enough to post about it on the Galactic Network—" He continued rambling, but India turned a sharp gaze in my direction. I utilized a tried-and-true tactic: ignoring her, even as sweat dampened my palms. "So the only other option is they tapped the *Calypso*, somehow."

Oh. Oh! Maybe it had nothing to do with me. Just an anonymous whaler hacking Mr. Hames's ship, stalking his progress for breakthroughs. I latched on to that theory, because *that* theory didn't make me the villain.

India had figured it out, though. She knew I'd reached out to Kane, knew I was hiding something now. India was a lot of things, but stupid wasn't one of them.

Even worse, Louisa leaned back in her chair to peer at me too. They'd *both* realized it. Facing India might kill me, but Louisa was an easy fix. I mustered up my fiercest glare, and she dropped her eyes to her holopad, face tinging red.

At the front of the room, Mr. Hames activated a few more display discs, then began dropping them around the room: a crude drawing of the star whale, with emphasis on its golden sails. Soon we were surrounded by the subject of my guilt.

Airtight, huh?

"Doesn't matter. They're here now, which means we need to move fast," Mr. Hames said. "And to do that, we have to think critically about the star whales. We know where to look for them, but—"

"Fast, because of the 'deadline'?" Tarynn asked loudly. When he paused, glancing at her, she crossed her arms. "We know all about the government grant, Mr. Hames."

I nearly snorted. Way to own information she'd just heard a few minutes ago.

Panic glinted in our teacher's eyes now, and he tugged at his collar. "Ah . . . found out about that, did you? Clever bunch."

"Max figured it out," Nashira said, jerking a thumb my way.

"Should have known." Mr. Hames sighed, looking straight at me now. I met his gaze defiantly, but my fingers dug into the plastic of my desk. He'd have to be a moron not to piece together the leak after I'd pressed him about Dad. About Kane. But if Mr. Hames realized what had happened, he didn't call me out. "To get the grant, you'd have to capture the whale. I—I did have hardware installed on the *Calypso* to do it, but after seeing them, I'd never use it."

"So you wanted the money," Rhett said.

Mr. Hames tilted his head. "Of course I did, but it was more than that. Whoever captures a star whale proves to the galaxy that they exist. It . . . well, it proves I'm not insane." Now a hint of a smile lifted his lips. "Should have known that was a fool's errand."

India chuckled.

Mr. Hames's gaze hardened as he strode toward the plastiglass windows, gesturing at the starships drifting around our space station. "Here's the thing, kids. The grant can't matter now, because *now* there are other whalers involved. If they find one, this weekend will become your new normal. Even after the deadline passes, they'll swarm Azura like rats, because there's no limit to the people who would pay to get a piece of a star whale."

I swallowed past the lump in my throat, imagining my home perpetually infested with whalers. Ms. Jakubowski's coffee shop, every table taken. The garden in the recreation level, trampled. The Galactic Network computers in the library, broken with overuse. Curfews in effect for all us kids, all the time.

And most importantly, who'd be responsible for recording their starships' coming and going? *Mom.* I'd barely seen her this weekend, and when she'd finally come home last night, it was with deep bags under her eyes and a pounding headache. She'd put leftovers on the table and collapsed on the couch for a nap.

And that would be our life . . . forever.

"If someone claims the grant, everyone will know the whales live nearby," I realized.

"They'll never stop hunting," Mr. Hames agreed. "If even one whaler discovers the truth, they'll devour everything that makes this place home for you kids. Azura will never be the same."

Silence. Everyone exchanged horrified glances. Guilt churned in my gut, tightening into nausea that only amplified when India shot me a look of betrayal. She wouldn't call me out, not in front of everyone, but the implication was clear.

I'd ruined Azura, unless we could stop it.

"So what's our plan?" Tarynn asked, taking command like always.

Mr. Hames rubbed the back of his neck. "Now that the whalers have a localized area to search, it's only a matter of time until someone sees through the whales' defenses. But if we can find them one more time, communicate through Max's music and convince them to leave the asteroid belt, they might stand a chance."

He looked at me, pleadingly. "What do you think, Max? Willing to give it a try?"

Of course I was. Anything to end this nightmare. I nodded.

Mr. Hames drew a deep breath. "Okay. Then our next issue becomes finding them quickly. Most whalers know about my ship. If we leave Azura, we'll be followed. My slipstream generator will give us a head start, but I'm not naive enough to think they won't catch up. Which means, for this plan to work, we have to find the whales *fast*. And you know what they say about knowledge and power."

He pointed at the images flickering around the room, determination evident in the set of his lips, the sharpness of his gaze. "It's time we have an open discussion about *stella cetacea*. I've been thinking about how a creature that big can sustain itself in space, and the only thing I'm coming up with is solar power." He pointed to the golden sails on the whale's back, and my eyes widened. Massive solar panels. Brilliant. "There *are* records of photosynthetic animals, although most of them are small, sea slugs and the like—"

From there, Mr. Hames became a real teacher, opening a scientific discussion with a class of kids. We brainstormed the possibility of *stella cetacea*'s solar sails, of the green divots on its nose that might be radiation sensors, of the wheat-like whiskers hovering over its blowhole that might recycle exhaled carbon dioxide in an environment with unbreathable, atomic oxygen.

After a while, Nashira said, "Yeah, but how do they affect the environment? Because before we scare them off, we should know that."

"You're absolutely right. I was thinking of other things unique to this area. It stands to reason a creature so unique would put something equally unique into the asteroid belt, right?" A grin formed on Mr. Hames's lips.

My jaw dropped. "The asteroid. The anemonium asteroids."

"Only found here, after all this time. Azura's nearly exhausted the supply, but every once in a while, you find a few new asteroids to mine." Mr. Hames strolled toward an old advertisement e-poster hanging on the wall. Propaganda from a century ago, promising riches and adventure to anyone brave enough to battle the frontier. Like an old gold rush, but far more lucrative.

Anemonium was one of the most revered materials in the galaxy, after all.

"What if they aren't asteroids?" Mr. Hames said, tapping the image on the poster. It showed the shiny asteroid, gleaming silver amid the gray rocks.

"*Silver means success,*" the e-poster read.

My brows knit together.

India drummed her fingers on the table. "What else would they be?"

Mr. Hames smirked. "Think about it. What would any organic creature leave behind?"

"Tracks?" Nashira suggested.

"Think . . . grosser." Mr. Hames seemed on the verge of laughter now.

"Oh, eww," Tarynn wrinkled her nose. "We're a bit old for that, Mr. Hames."

Arsenio forced his expression from delighted to carefully neutral, and I stifled a chuckle. Mr. Hames winked. "It's a fact of life, Tarynn. But what if, in the vacuum of space, their excrement hardens the way minerals do deep underground?"

"So all this time, we've been mining . . . poop." Rhett sounded horrified.

Well, that'd explain why the whale didn't want to touch that particular asteroid.

India grinned. "Airtight."

I stared at the e-poster as everything clicked into place. Azura's supply started dwindling about two decades ago, marking the end of one of the most successful mining expeditions in history. Our space station quickly fell into obscurity, but Dad used to comment on how weird the anemonium asteroids were. How it was so strange they weren't spread across the entire asteroid belt, but rather concentrated here.

Did he know?

Or had Mr. Hames just cracked a code even Dad couldn't puzzle through?

"It stands to reason," I said, regaining Mr. Hames's attention, "that if we want to find a star whale fast, all we'd have to do is track down the highest concentration of anemonium asteroids."

"Exactly." Mr. Hames snapped his fingers.

"The mineships have a program to localize the best spots to find anemonium," Nashira offered. "Louisa could mimic that program on the *Calypso*."

Her sister nodded, meekly. "S-sure."

Mr. Hames surveyed us all, clearly pleased. "Well, then. Sounds like we have a battle plan."

17

AZURA'S PLIGHT

After class, as we filed out, Mr. Hames said, "Ah, Max? A word?"

Stars, this was it. He *did* know about me and Kane. I flinched, glancing at India for help, but she just shrugged. I mean, I couldn't blame her; she'd been so excited about boarding a real starship, seeing what else was out there, and I'd gone and ruined it. The ramifications of the whalers were *very* clear: we'd get one more excursion. Just one more adventure, and then if all went well, the whales would move on—hopefully not forever, but long enough we might never see them again—and we'd return to our boring, normal lives on the space station Azura.

And that was my fault.

So when she abandoned me to Mr. Hames's lecture, it was nothing I didn't deserve. But it still hurt, watching her leave without a word. As the door slid shut, I faced my executioner.

Mr. Hames walked to the side of his desk, leaning against it like he had the first day of class. But this time, he wasn't floundering for something to say. This time, disappointment settled over his face.

I pressed my lips together, defenses already forming in my mind. The *Enrapture* hadn't been seen on Azura yet, so maybe

Kane wasn't behind this. Besides, Mr. Hames couldn't prove I'd told Kane, not unless he hacked my messages, and wow, that'd be a breach of privacy.

But flimsy as those excuses were, I didn't need to use them. He shocked me by saying instead, "I'm sorry, Max. This is my fault."

Wait. "What?"

Mr. Hames heaved a sigh, gripping the corners of the desk. "That day in the cargo bay, when you confronted me about being a whaler . . . I should have told you about the government grant, but I didn't."

This was about the grant? I swallowed hard but didn't dare interrupt.

He lowered his gaze. "You were so mad at me. And this dark part of my brain whispered that if I told you the truth, if you thought I was only here for the money, you wouldn't fix the Starkwil generator. And then I'd be stranded on Azura." Shame tinged his ears deep red. "That's why I'm sorry, Max. I used you, and that was wrong. None of this should have been your problem. Not the generator, not *stella cetacea*, not the whalers. I'm sorry you have to deal with it."

He really hadn't put two and two together, had he? He didn't realize what I'd done. The silence was heavy, his admission hanging between us. If I opened my mouth to accept it, I'd have to come clean about my flaw too.

And I couldn't do it. I couldn't just admit this was my fault. So I sat there, awkwardly, until Mr. Hames forced a smile.

"We get one shot at this, Max," he said, pushing off the

desk. "One shot to make it right. All we have to do is find the star whales again. You with me?"

I nodded quietly.

Silently.

He ruffled my hair. "Okay. Then spread the word. Tomorrow morning, we meet at the *Calypso*."

"Okay," I said, and when he turned back to the holographic images of the crudely drawn star whales, I hightailed it out of Classroom 7.

———————

To my surprise, India was waiting outside. She pushed off the wall, crossing her arms in a shockingly good impression of Tarynn. I tried to smile, to wave, but she wasn't having it.

"That was a pretty short conversation, considering the topic. Did he lecture you on stranger danger?"

Hang on. India was the one person on Azura who should understand what I was going through. We were the two fatherless kids. The ones desperate to know anything about them, even something as simple as the fact that my dad had played an instrument or that hers liked to travel. Even if we didn't talk about them much, they were always there, weighing on our minds.

And now she was acting like that didn't make a stars-darned difference. Like what I'd done, talking to Kane, was completely unsanctioned.

I clenched my fists. "No, he didn't lecture me. Kane's not a stranger. He's my dad's best friend."

India barked a laugh. "Max, we're best friends. Kane is, at

best, a friend your dad once had. And you just went and *told him* the one thing Mr. Hames warned us not to spread around. Almost like he knew all these whalers would follow the gossip."

"Everyone follows gossip," I snapped, plucking the smoke bomb she'd tucked into my jacket pocket. It gleamed blue and white, the size of a marble, and her eyes latched on to it. "Why do you think we used a smoke bomb when Mr. Hames's starship was towed into Azura?"

"That has nothing to do with this, because *that* was harmless."

"Gossip is never harmless." I shoved the marble back into my pocket. "And smoke bombs certainly aren't. You heard Mrs. Smith coughing the next day. That wasn't just age." Was that true? No idea. But it carved a handhold in this argument. India paled, which made me feel like I was winning, so I pressed on. "You're the reason Mr. Bruska broke his leg too. He had to go to the inner planets for therapy. His whole life disrupted because of a prank. How's that for harmless?"

Tears sprang to India's eyes, but they weren't sad tears. No, these were angry, making her scathing gaze shine like ice. "You and I both did that prank, Max. And unlike you, I already apologized to Mr. Bruska. Mom went with me to the hospital; we brought him flowers from the garden and everything. I asked you to come, and what did you say? You 'had to work' at Mr. Keller's shop." The air quotes stabbed my heart, but her frigid tone was worse. "Were you ever employed there, or was that another lie?"

"Of course I work there!" I was digging myself deeper, but I couldn't stop arguing. Couldn't stop defending myself. "I need to repair Dad's decivox. You know that."

"All I know is that you yelled at Mr. Hames for lying, and now, two weeks later, you're doing it yourself. And that's not the Maxion I'm friends with."

I stiffened. "Well, the India *I* like is perfectly happy to live here, on Azura, forever! What happened to her?"

"She's gone! Okay? I've already talked to Mom about it, and guess what? She's tired of this space station too. She said, once I hit sixteen, we can move somewhere else. But now I'm wondering why we should wait!"

The blood drained from my face, and a chill flashed across my body. India, my best friend since forever . . . leaving? I knew she wanted to travel, but I'd never imagined her mom would go along with it. Mine certainly wouldn't. We were Azurans.

But without India, what was the point of staying?

Anguish made me growl, "Fine, then. Do it. Move to the inner planets and swim like a mermaid or gape at a really big tree or *drown* in hundreds of new cultures. Go to a whole new star system, for all I care!"

"Maybe I will!" she shouted.

"Kids," a stern voice said behind us, and we both spun to see Mr. Hames standing at the door to his classroom. His brows knitted together. For a second, I was terrified he'd heard about what I'd done with Kane, but he just asked, "Something wrong?"

"No," we both answered at once.

India glared at me. I scowled back.

"Everything's fine, Mr. Hames. See you tomorrow," she muttered.

"Bright and early in Hangar 42," he replied, cautiously, as if he was perched between two rabid dogs.

She nodded and, without even a glance at me, stomped down the corridor to the central lifts. I waved at Mr. Hames and sulked after her, but when I got there, the doors had already shut.

India was gone.

18

KANE AND THE BOX

I barely slept that night, thinking about what I'd done. What I'd said, to India and Kane and Mr. Hames. After hours of tossing and turning, I finally drifted into a nightmarish sleep where India and her mom boarded a mineship like the one that killed Dad, jettisoned into space, only to have Kane intercept them. They were swallowed by the *Enrapture*, suddenly the size of a star whale. Mr. Hames appeared in the *Calypso* and tried to rescue them, but before he could, everything exploded.

I gasped awake, sweating and shaking.

Mom wasn't around when I staggered out of my bedroom. She must have gone to work early, a common issue now that the whalers were everywhere. Numbly, I made oatmeal, watching the clock inch closer to the start of school.

For a brief moment, I toyed with the idea of ditching. I wouldn't even have to fake the stomachache this time; my gut had been churning for days. I clenched my eyes shut and pushed away the bowl of oatmeal. It'd be easy to stay home, but the class needed me. The *star whales* needed me.

With a heavy sigh, I headed to the hangar level.

I expected the class to be there, waiting. I expected Mr. Hames to be performing a last-minute walkaround of the *Calypso*, discussing fudged flight plans with Nashira and hangar hacks with Louisa. I expected Tarynn would want to know why I was late, and Rhett would want to know why my shirt clearly hadn't been washed in a few days, and Arsenio would offer a smile I didn't feel like returning. I expected India would be so furious, she probably wouldn't even talk to me.

What I didn't expect was Kane.

It felt like I'd been punched in the stomach. I froze, eyes widening, heart stuttering, but there was no mistaking it. His blond mustache and buzz-cut hair were impossible to misidentify, even if the wrinkles around his eyes and mouth had aged him.

It was only a matter of time, my mind whispered, traitorously.

No, I thought back, feeling far younger than my twelve years. *No, it's not fair. This isn't my fault.*

He was talking with Mr. Hames just a few feet from the *Calypso*. I ghosted to the back of the class, eyes glued to their exchange. Everyone, even Tarynn, had fallen silent, watching the whalers from afar.

Whatever they were saying, Kane was clearly amused. He laughed boisterously, clapping Mr. Hames's shoulder. Our teacher brushed him off, then took a step backward.

A few feet away, I noticed India. Maybe she knew how upset I was, how angry and scared and betrayed. Maybe she'd forgiven me after all.

But she didn't move toward me. Instead, she glowered, then whispered something in Louisa's ear. The mousy girl clutched her holopad to her chest, lips pressing together. The implication was obvious. Theirs wasn't a sudden friendship; it was a meeting of mutual parties with a common goal.

A common enemy.

Me.

But they didn't say anything, despite the rest of our class standing nearby. Of course, they didn't need to, because one minute later Kane saw me and grinned widely. By the way he yelled, everyone on Azura must have heard.

"You must be Maxion Belmont! Look at you, little man. Milo, ain't he the spitting image of his dad?"

It was like the entire class tensed as one. As Kane strolled to meet me, shaking my hand with enough strength to pinch my fingers, my friends glared, murmuring under their breaths, and quietly labeled me the villain of this story.

Fear crippled me, fear that I could never make this better, could never *fix* this problem. My hydrodriver was useless here. My decivox couldn't soothe this issue. On a space station where everyone knew my name, what if I was suddenly . . . alone? Worse, surrounded by people who hated me?

I'd just wanted to learn more about my dad. Why was that so much to ask?

I couldn't even look Kane in the eyes. I wrenched my hand away, fighting to keep my breathing steady, fighting to stave off the tears. My hands shook, and I shoved them into my pocket, brushing India's smoke bomb.

A distant part of me longed to throw it and *run*.

I didn't.

Meanwhile, Mr. Hames strolled over to us, swiftly positioning himself between the class and Kane. He put a hand on my shoulder, which made me flinch. But he didn't tighten his grip, didn't glare at me or accuse me or *anything*.

Instead, he whispered, "I know you didn't mean it, Max."

But I *did* mean it. That was the worst part.

Without waiting for a reply, he faced Kane, a physical barrier between us. "I told you. I'm not a whaler anymore, Kingston. I'm a teacher now."

"Hames, come on. After all we've been through, you're still going to lie to me?" Kane pressed a hand to his chest, mock offended. Mr. Hames frowned, but Kane then gestured at me, offering a wry smile. "Look, Max told me everything. I just want to see them for myself. Is that so wrong?"

A few of my classmates muttered behind me, dark and dangerous. Every word was like a dagger to the heart. A room incrementally losing oxygen, and soon enough I wouldn't be able to breathe.

Mr. Hames pressed his lips into a firm line. "Sorry, Kane. Max was mistaken. Look at where we are; Azura's in the middle of nowhere. If the star whales were here—"

"—it'd be pretty easy to hide them," Kane replied, almost suspicious.

"I don't know what to tell you. Feel free to go look, but you won't find much." Mr. Hames shrugged.

Please believe it. Please leave us alone.

Kane's gaze shifted to me. Although his expression was curious, inquisitive, his eyes seemed to pierce my soul.

Mr. Hames took advantage of the silence, pointing at the

Calypso. "Come on, kids. Class starts in ten, and I expect you all at your stations before then. If you'll excuse us, Kingston, we have a lesson."

Kane drawled, "A lesson in the asteroid belt?"

Mr. Hames slipped smoothly into his lie, laughing loud and amused. "Stars, no. Do you really think their parents would let me kidnap a class of children for a joyride? Kane, your brain must be blackened, staring into space all that time. You're losing it." Still chuckling, he shooed our class toward the *Calypso.*

"You heard him. Move it," Tarynn ordered, and everyone filed out.

Everyone except me. I took one step, and Kane called, "Max, wait."

And I stopped. India was a few steps away, gesturing for me to follow her, but—I stopped. Because no matter how angry I was at Kane for brushing me off, for inviting the whalers, for instigating this whole mess . . . he was still the last connection to my dad.

And if he had something to say, I needed to know.

I *had* to know.

"Max," Mr. Hames said, a warning in his voice. "Class is starting soon."

The whales were counting on us. But the sooner we got rid of Kane, the sooner we could leave, and he clearly wasn't exiting Hangar 42 until we talked. Besides, I had a few questions myself. I waved Mr. Hames off and strolled to Kane. I was so tired, I could *feel* the bags under my eyes, feel the weight in my limbs, and every inch of me was aware it was his fault.

My tone was sharper than intended, but nothing less than he deserved. "I just wanted to talk to you about my dad." My eyes burned again, mentioning him, so I glared instead. Being angry meant I wasn't sad. One was definitely preferable. "Just a few conversations. That's it!"

"I want that too," Kane said, almost desperate. "Damian was a great guy, and I was proud to offer you some insight."

"Then why? Why come all this way, when we could have just talked on the Galactic Network? Why bring all the other whalers with you?" I left the deeper question out: *How could you do this to me?*

His expression darkened. "The whalers coming here was a mistake. My programmer found our messages and released the information . . . for a fee. He ain't on the *Enrapture* anymore. Promise, Max. I only want to see the star whales for myself."

"You want to get the grant for yourself."

"No reason we shouldn't be paid for the discovery," Kane said, running a hand over his buzz cut. "Your father and I used to fantasize about what we'd do with that money. I bet Hames does too."

Mr. Hames, standing beside me, stiffened. Despite the accusation, he kept silent, letting me have this conversation.

"I came all this way to find the whales, yes, but also to meet *you*, Max," Kane continued, a smile spreading across his face. "You know what I found in storage? A box of your dad's old stuff. It's everything he left on the *Enrapture*. He'd have wanted you to have it."

My skin turned ice cold. Living on a space station, Azurans

didn't keep many tangible items. There just wasn't room to store it all, so I'd spent my life being picky about what I owned. Dad was the same, and when he died, Mom threw out almost everything . . . everything except his hydrodriver and his decivox.

Now there was a whole new box of things, like a time capsule into my father's life.

And Kane had made the trip all the way to Azura, just to give it to me. Stars, that was . . . amazing.

"That's kind of you," Mr. Hames said, but the skepticism in his tone made me scowl.

Kane heard it too. He rolled his eyes. "Don't be like that, Milo. I got a crew to feed, and that's expensive, so of course I'm headin' to the asteroid belt. But ain't no reason I can't also give Max here something of Damian's first."

"Where is it? Do you have it?" I asked, desperately.

"Well, not here," Kane admitted. "It's a big box."

A thrill raced through me. A *big* box? What kinds of things had Dad kept during his teenage years? This was better than the hydrodriver, which I'd seen him using all my life. No, this was identical to when I found the decivox in my parents' closet, weeks after Dad died, and realized a whole new facet of his life.

It had become such a big facet of mine in the years since. What mysteries would be unveiled in that box, talents pursued and hobbies entertained and interests explored? What else could I learn about Dad—and myself—with those items?

Suddenly, another thought occurred to me. It had always struck me as odd that Dad never had a repair kit for his instrument.

He fixed everything else himself, so why hadn't I found tools to reattach his decivox's metal rod?

Unless he'd forgotten it on the *Enrapture*. My heart raced. "Wait, did you look inside? Did you see any repair kits?"

Kane's brows furrowed. "Ah, there might have been something like that. Tiny black case? Sleek metal?"

I had no idea what a decivox repair kit looked like, but that *had* to be it. After all this time, two years of working at Mr. Keller's shop, and Kane would be the reason I finally fixed that instrument. Excitement tinged my voice. "Can I come get it?"

"'Course you can!" Kane grinned. "But it'll have to be soon. We're leaving for the asteroid belt in a few."

Mr. Hames gripped my shoulder again, and this time his fingers tightened warningly. He didn't have to speak; I knew what that meant. If we didn't beat Kane and the *Enrapture* there, if I didn't dismiss the star whales before he found them, Azura would never be the same. My life and my classmates', changed forever.

But that box was a physical connection to my dad, and I couldn't just ignore it. I missed him *so* much. I wanted to hold the things he'd held, pursue the things he'd loved. What was so bad about that?

I gasped, desperate, "What about later tonight, or tomorrow? I—I have class now."

Kane's eyes settled on Mr. Hames's hand, and he sighed, shaking his head. "Listen, Max, we can't stick around. If this don't pan out, we have to follow some other leads. Time's tickin'. But if you come back with me now, I'll be quick. Milo, you can spare him for a few, right?"

"No, actually." Mr. Hames's voice was uncharacteristically hard. "Come along, Max. Everyone's waiting."

Yeah. My classmates, my friends . . . who all hated me right now. I clenched my eyes shut. What did I do? Forsake the whales for Dad's box? Or leave it behind and save a species?

Before I could decide, a hand snaked into mine, squeezed. India. She stood on my other side, seeming taller than the trees in the botanarium. Her eyes flashed at Kane, but she smiled prettily and said, "I have a solution. Why can't you just leave the box with Max's mom? She works on this level. She's around here somewhere."

Wait. *Wait.* That was perfect! I grinned, squeezing India's hand back. "Yeah! I can call her. She could probably beat you to the *Enrapture*. And she'd love a box of Dad's stuff." A lie; Mom couldn't really look at Dad's old things—that's why she threw most of them out. Pictures were all she could handle, and even they made her tear up sometimes.

"There we go," Mr. Hames said, smirking now. "How about it, Kane? Everyone wins."

Kane faltered. "Ah, sure. Sure." He tilted his head, then nodded. "Actually, I can call her myself. No need to interrupt your 'lesson.' If you change your mind, though, Max, I'm in Hangar 13." With a wave, he strolled toward the docking level's circular hallway.

Hangar 13. A box of my dad's things, including a bona fide repair kit for his decivox, was waiting just down the hall. And even though Mom would collect the box, I wanted to be the first to open it.

And yet, I had other priorities.

But when I turned to thank India, she dropped my hand. "I can't believe you trusted that guy. What a sleaze." With a scoff, she stomped to the *Calypso*.

I stood dumbstruck, numb. Stupid me, thinking her intervention meant she'd forgiven me. Nooo. Apparently, she just thought I needed a babysitter.

Irritation burned my chest, but she was gone before I could say anything.

Mr. Hames sighed, rubbing his arm. "Come on, Max. We have somewhere to be."

Unfortunately, he was right. With nothing else to do, I followed him.

19

THE BLOOD OF A FIGHT

Mr. Hames slapped a button near the top of the *Calypso*'s curved staircase, and the whole thing lifted off the floor of Hangar 42, sealing us inside his starship. He checked to make sure I was still beside him, then hollered orders at the waiting kids.

"India, head to the flight deck, please. We need to get this starship spaceborne sooner than later. Nashira, fudge that transmission to the space traffic controller. Louisa, get our cover story in place. It probably won't help, but we can try."

India stomped down the hallway without a word, then climbed the spiral staircase to the upper deck.

Whatever. Why would I want to hang out with someone who couldn't even give me the benefit of the doubt? She was supposed to be my friend, but she hadn't even asked *why* I'd told Kane in the first place. It was like she didn't care.

Fine by me. I didn't care about her either.

"Um, Mr. Hames?" Arsenio asked.

Our teacher heaved a sigh but stopped his panicked run to focus on the medic. "Yes? What's wrong?"

"Um, I was thinking last night. Won't sending the whales away . . . hurt Azura?" Everyone in the cargo bay paused, heads swiveling toward Arsenio. He looked vastly uncomfortable, tugging at his apron. "It's just—we only make money by exporting the little amounts of anemonium we can still find. And typically, when the supply dries up, mining towns turn into—" He swallowed. "G-ghost towns."

Mr. Hames scrubbed his face. "I know. But if the whales have lived here since Azura was founded, I doubt they'd leave for good. The space station *might* suffer in the distant future, but if we don't act now, our immediate future is worse."

"Plus, if the whalers find these whales, they'll be hunted . . . maybe to extinction. And then we still won't have anemonium to mine," I said.

Everyone glared at me, and I hunched against their ire, skin prickling in shame, heart clenching in anger. Probably, I shouldn't be talking about dire consequences when *I* called everyone here in the first place.

But it still wasn't fair.

But Mr. Hames nodded, smoothly moving us along. "Right. The benefits outweigh the potential risks. Does everyone agree with that?"

Murmurs of approval rippled through the class. Mr. Hames clapped his hands together, casting a dubious glance at the closed cargo bay door. "Okay. Kane's running back to his starship now, and if he beats us to space, it'll be a lot easier to track where we went. We have to get out of Azura before he gets the chance."

"So, he *can* track us?" Tarynn demanded, shooting me a pointed stare. I scowled, pressing against the curved bulkhead wall of the cargo bay.

Mr. Hames ran a hand through his hair. "He can try. With

my slipstream generator, we're faster than any of their ships, but it'll only buy us an hour or two. Once Kane gets to the asteroid belt, his scanners won't have a problem finding us. Get to the flight deck, guys."

With determined nods, Louisa and Nashira sprinted after India. Mr. Hames followed, only pausing to spare me one last disappointed glance.

I hated the way he looked at me. How Tarynn and Rhett muttered under their breaths after he left, how I caught the word "Max" filled with malice. I hated everything about this situation. I'd never felt so trapped, back against the wall, locked on a ship of unfriendly faces. Well, mostly unfriendly faces—and Arsenio, who scrubbed his palms on his medical apron, expression conflicted.

I could have had a friend in him if I hadn't been so mean.

Too little, too late. I'd made a mistake boarding the *Calypso*. I bet Mr. Hames could play the decivox well enough to send the whales away. I bet they didn't even need me.

My eyes flicked to the red button beside the folded staircase. Was it too late to leave? I could probably still catch Kane, get that box, and spend the rest of the day in my apartment, unpacking Dad's old things.

Stars, nothing sounded better. But—but everyone here was counting on me. If I left now . . .

That's when Tarynn stomped up to me, her gaze piercing. "You really messed up, Max."

I squared my shoulders, but it was hard to be defiant when I just felt sick and sad. I wished India was here.

"Yeah. Never pegged you for a snitch," Rhett added with a sneer, moving shoulder to shoulder with Tarynn.

The floor began to tremble as the slipstream generator powered on. I'd waited too long. The hangar's airlock would be closing, which meant no turning back. Slammed with that realization, facing their hostility, I felt faint. I needed to get away, needed to get Mr. Hames's stupid decivox and play until I forgot how terrible today was.

The engine room. At least I could hide in the engine room.

I tried to step around them, but Rhett shoved my shoulders.

My heel hit the folded staircase sealed against the cargo bay's grated floor, and I careened backward, falling hard. My head smacked against one of its stairs, and white burst behind my eyes. The shock of pain made me gasp.

"Max!" Arsenio exclaimed.

Rhett loomed over me. "That'll teach you," he muttered, smoothing his jacket.

Tarynn stood behind him, arms crossed, expression dark. "If we didn't need your music, you wouldn't even *be* here. Got it?"

"You hurt him," Arsenio exclaimed, uncharacteristically angry. He pushed past Rhett, kneeling to squint at my head, holding a finger in front of my eyes. Like I had a concussion or something from one little fall.

"He deserved it," Rhett snapped.

Arsenio glowered at him, venom in his tone. "No one deserves that! And you guys are forgetting that without Max's engineering skills, *none* of us would be here. None of us would have even *seen* the whales." He offered me a hand. "Are you okay, Max?"

But I couldn't move.

They hated me. After over a decade of knowing them, of being in their class, one little mistake had changed their entire opinion of me. Just because I wanted more information about my dad. Just because I missed him so much it ached, felt like a star imploding, left me a shell of who I used to be.

Arsenio was trying to be nice, but that was ridiculous. Nothing about my actions in the last two weeks—no, the last two *years*—implied I was someone worth knowing. And he kept trying, even now, even while everyone else saw me for what I was.

A fraud. A snitch.

A liar.

"Leave me alone," I gasped, and shoved Arsenio's hand away. He backed off but almost immediately backpedaled into our teacher, who'd strolled into the cargo bay with all the indignation of an oncoming storm.

"What's going on here?" Mr. Hames exclaimed, aghast.

"Rhett pushed Max," Arsenio said, as if he was being *so* helpful.

Rhett's cheeks colored. "No! He fell."

Mr. Hames crossed his arms. His voice remained level, but somehow it seemed louder than shouting. "Care to try that answer again?"

Rhett flinched. "H-he deserved it." It sounded feeble now, faced with our teacher's scrutiny. "He ratted us out, Mr. Hames! That Kane guy is only following us because of him."

Mr. Hames didn't speak for or against that statement. He just shook his head and uncrossed his arms, staring down at them. "I expected better from you, Rhett. You of all people should know that violence never solves problems. And *you*, Tarynn. You're our first officer. How can you condone this?"

Tarynn's face went deep red, and she scuffed the grated floor. For the first time in her life, she didn't have anything to say.

Mr. Hames frowned. "Go on. All of you. Upstairs."

They shuffled away, but I couldn't even feel smug about it. Everything was numb, surreal. Tarynn couldn't meet my gaze as they turned, trudging up the spiral staircase out of sight.

Arsenio, on the other hand, hesitated near the hallway's entrance. "Mr. Hames, I can help—"

"I know you can, Arsenio," he replied with a tired smile. "But I think Max wants to be alone for a minute. If we need you, we'll come to the medbay, okay?"

"O-okay," Arsenio said. "Feel better, Max."

I couldn't even reply as he followed them upstairs, leaving Mr. Hames and me alone. The idea of facing Rhett and Tarynn and everyone else, of facing *India*, had me trembling. The back of my head pounded, making me think that maybe I *did* have a concussion. I picked myself up off the floor, gingerly touching the back of my head.

"I'm so sorry, Max," Mr. Hames was saying, hovering close enough to catch me if I fell. "I should have been here. I never thought—"

Through my curly hair, my fingers touched something tacky and wet. Oh. I'd hit the stairs hard enough to draw blood. *W-was that my first fight?* Panic welled as I smeared the dark red between my fingers. Like grease, only smoother, warmer. Rhett had pushed me, and Tarynn had cheered, and Arsenio had just been trying to help, and India was nowhere to be seen—and all the while, the Starkwil generator was warming up, and the departure codes were being sent to Kaito. The asteroid belt and the star whales beckoned, and I was about to be stuck on this starship, *stuck* with the same people who muttered about me, glowered at me, pushed me, when I could have followed Kane and collected Dad's box and spent the afternoon in the quiet peace of our home—and deep inside my mind, something snapped.

"Let me out," I said hollowly.

Mr. Hames had just noticed the blood on my fingers. "Oh, *Max.* Hang on. I'll get some bandages—"

He hadn't heard me. Or he had, and he wasn't listening. I wiped the blood on my black pants, on the uniform I no longer wanted to wear. The starship rumbled, and we were about to go into space, and I just *couldn't* be trapped here with my classmates.

This time, I yelled it.

"I said, *Let me out!*"

Mr. Hames froze, eyes widening. "Max, you're hurt. I can help—"

"No, you can't," I snarled. "*Kane* helped. You just used me. Stars, you're still using me. First for the slipstream generator and then to find the whales! You told me you were sorry, but that was just another lie, wasn't it?"

"You can't trust Kane, Max."

Warm blood trickled down my neck, sending goose bumps

over my arms. I clenched my fists. "I trust him more than I trust you! At least I can get some answers about Dad by talking to him. At least he doesn't let kids push me around."

Mr. Hames stiffened, falling silent. A moment of contemplation, and then—then he did what adults do when they're forced to face their own actions. He deflected. "Max, sit down. Let me look at that wound."

But I was done. In another minute, the starship would lift off, exit the airlock doors, and rocket toward the asteroid belt, and I couldn't be a part of that. Panic hardened into one thought: *move!*

So I did. I shoved past him, slapped the red button to disengage the staircase, and leapt on it as it hissed open. Hangar 42's airlock hadn't sealed yet, hadn't started the decompression process—the stairs never would have opened if it had—but twenty feet away, the doors were closing.

Time was ticking.

"Max!" Mr. Hames lunged for me, but I ducked away, staggering off the stairs and landing with a *thump* on the floor of the hangar. He moved to follow me, then froze, glancing over his shoulder at the staircase. He had our whole class under his supervision. If he left now, the *Calypso* might seal them inside without him. Already, the staircase was lifting back into the belly of his starship.

Already, it was too late to follow.

"Max, please," he begged. For what, I wasn't sure. Even if I wanted to, which I didn't, I'd never make it back onto the starship in time.

And if I didn't get past the huge airlock doors before they sealed, I'd be dead in minutes.

I *ran*, my breath hitching as I darted through the dwindling crack between the massive doors, gasping as they slammed shut behind me. Through the plastiglass windows, the staircase melded flush with the bullet-shaped hull of the *Calypso*. Everything went silent as I held my breath, waiting to see if Mr. Hames would cancel the launch, would order the airlock doors open to retrieve me.

But he'd always said he wouldn't force us into space.

A moment later, the airlock blared a warning, and the outer set of doors opened into space, releasing the *Calypso* from Azura's hold.

In minutes, they were gone.

20

THE ELUSIVE BOX

Two steps outside Hangar 42, I froze. The hallways bustled with strangers—whalers—so congested I had to flatten against the bulkhead just to avoid getting trampled. They shouted and synced holopads with pinprick cameras hidden along the massive corridor and scurried back to their respective ships. At least some of them had seen the *Calypso* leaving and discerned what it meant.

My class wouldn't have much time.

I didn't either. A ship of a hundred people would take a while to mobilize, but Kane would be following as soon as he could. There was no guarantee he'd called my mom to collect that box. Hangar 13 was on the other side of Azura, so I picked up my pace, sprinting through the circular hallway. All I had to do was get to Kane's ship and I'd have Dad's repair kit.

I could fix his decivox.

Everything would be fine.

Except . . . wait. The decivox. The whalers were all over Azura, like an infestation of ants, strangers filling every corner of our home looking for a quick digit. Fear gripped me. All this time, I'd never thought about my dad's decivox, sitting unattended in that storage shed. It was a pretty rare instrument; what if the whalers found it and realized its worth? What if someone had already stolen my most prized possession?

My heart seized, and then I was running in the other direction, toward the central lifts. Kane had promised to call Mom anyway, but that decivox only had me. Dad's hydrodriver was heavy in my pocket as I weaved between the whalers, strange men and women who chuckled and shouted as I sprinted past, as I called an elevator and dove inside.

"Where's the fire?" one called after me as the doors slid shut.

Jerks. All of them. My chest tightened as I thought of them disrupting our quiet, calm space station. But it wasn't up to me anymore. I'd only ruined things. Mr. Hames and my class were the last ones who could fix it.

I just had to pray one of them could play his decivox well enough to shoo the star whales from the asteroid belt.

The recreation level was almost as busy, if that was possible. Ms. Jakubowski had deep bags under her eyes, forcing smiles for men who crooned at her and waved their mugs over their heads. Maria and her daughter, Rose, were gone, as were most of the other Azurans. The whalers had taken every court, every chess table, every VR simulator. They oozed through the space like a toxin.

My heart leapt into my throat as one approached the storage shed.

"Hey!" I shouted. The whaler, a thin man with a beard, spun toward me. Thinking fast, I lowered my voice as I got closer. "Ah, didn't you hear? They saw a star whale near the Kialoa Nebula. If you guys hang out here, you're going to miss it."

"How did you know—" He cut himself off, eyes widening. "Never mind. Thanks, kid!" And with a shout, he waved at his friends, gesturing to the central lifts. A few of them broke off, acting subtle as they slunk into the elevators.

I didn't even have the energy to smile. It wouldn't buy much time, and Kane would still head to the asteroid belt, in the opposite direction—following the *Calypso*—any minute. If I wanted to get that box, I had to move fast. But first . . .

The old, rusted lock unhooked beneath my fingers, and I wrenched the door open, sliding to my knees in the dusty room. For a terrifying moment while my eyes adjusted, I couldn't find the black case. My hands swam through the darkness, and—there! It hadn't been stolen. It was right where I'd left it after my last concert for India.

I paused, hands trembling as I popped open the black case, tracing the soft wood of the instrument inside. India had sat on that netting just two weeks ago, listening and laughing and applauding. I'd tried so hard to convince her Azura was the place to be, and she—she'd left anyway. Today was just the first solo excursion in a future brimming with them.

I swallowed hard. Even if I wanted to see the galaxy, I'd blown it. I'd messed up, shared something that wasn't mine to tell, and run away. Of course they'd left me behind. They had a mission, and . . . I had a box of Dad's stuff.

Feeling more miserable than ever, neck itching from the drying blood, I hugged the decivox case to my chest and left the storage shed behind.

———

The elevator doors opened on the hangar level for the second time that morning, and I leapt into the hallway. The wonky gravity settled as I sprinted toward the outer corridor, veering away from Hangar 42.

I'd barely taken one step, however, when Mom's voice intoned over the level-wide intercom: "Maxion Cameron Belmont. Repeat, Maxion Cameron Belmont. Report to the hangar offices immediately."

My face burned. Stars, calling me over the intercoms? They only used those for, like, toddlers who got lost. How embarrassing.

Did she know I'd abandoned my class? No, she couldn't. Because that would mean Mr. Hames had called her, and then he'd have to come clean about their unsanctioned trip to the asteroid belt, and that'd put him in so much trouble.

He wouldn't risk it. Right?

"Maxion Belmont. Repeat. Report to the hangar offices. *Now*, young man."

I flinched, even as the whalers nearby laughed boisterously. "Someone's in trouuu-ble," one sang, and I ducked my head and stomped away. That wasn't an "I got your dad's box and want to show you" kind of message. That was a "you're grounded until you die" message.

Which meant Kane's box was still on the *Enrapture*.

Only about a half hour had passed since the *Calypso* took off. There might still be time to retrieve it. With Mom's message droning overhead, I sprinted away from the offices in question, right to Hangar 13.

Right to Kane.

The hallway doors were closed when I arrived. My heart dropped; closed doors meant the airlock was activating. The ship was leaving. And Dad's box was leaving with them. "No!" I exclaimed, banging my fist against the door. "No, please."

Wait. Protocol kept the door closed, but I knew the override. Of course! Ignoring the curious stares of the whalers nearby, I skidded to the security panel, setting the decivox case at my knees. In seconds, my hydrodriver was whirring to life in my hands. The panel popped off, and I got a serious case of déjà vu as I pried past the wires inside to find the override switch.

This time, I got to press it.

This time, the doors clicked open, and Mom wasn't waiting beyond them.

Of course, she'd seen the notification, because the moment I pushed to my feet, Kaito the space traffic controller's watery voice filled the intercom. "Max, your mother's on her way. If I were you, I'd stay put."

Oh stars. I was really playing with fire here. Tugging at my collar, head pounding, heart thumping, I pocketed the hydrodriver, snatched the decivox case, and ran into the hangar.

But the *Enrapture* hadn't left yet. The airlock doors weren't closed. People still bustled outside, hollering orders, nearly ready for launch. And the ship behind them had me frozen in place, jaw dropping.

Hangar 13 was easily five times the size of Hangar 42, and the *Enrapture* still barely fit. This was the hangar where Mom and Kaito usually corralled Azura's monthly aid shipment, all the food and supplies we couldn't produce for ourselves, sent straight from the inner planets. That freighter had to be big, since it distributed supplies to four or five space stations like ours. But it was still only half the size of the starship before me.

I racked my brain to identify it but fell short. All my research, and I'd never thought to find a picture of the *Enrapture* from the outside. Unlike the *Calypso*'s bullet shape, this was closer to a big, ugly rectangle. Its flight deck was built into the base, and a side staircase led into the belly of the cargo bay. Escape pods bubbled the back of it, like a bunch of grapes stuck in peanut butter. Through the wide bank of windows, people jogged past like they had somewhere vital to be.

On the ground outside the starship, more crew scurried about, checking fuel chambers and exhaust vents. If those photos India and I had found were any indication, the *Enrapture* had a crew complement of one hundred people, leagues above the *Calypso*'s eight. Would I even find Kane amid that chaos?

Well, I'd have to. Because they were leaving, and Mom was on her way, and if I didn't get that box before she got here, I might never get the chance again. I sucked in a breath and ran for the nearest crew member.

He was a short, stout man, barking orders at the other people outside the ship, and he glanced at me in disdain. "What are you doing here? You're lost, boy. Go home."

"Ah . . ."

"Well, spit it out."

Dad wasn't much older than me when he joined this ship's crew. He would never have stammered in the face of authority.

He always sounded so confident, smiled with such ease. *Channel Dad.* "I'm looking for Kane. He has something of mine."

The man raised an eyebrow, eyes flicking to the case in my hands. I gripped it tighter, keeping my expression stoic until he scoffed. "Hang on." And he stomped up the staircase, disappearing into the *Enrapture*.

I glanced over my shoulder, half expecting Mom to storm in any minute and silence everyone. But it only took a few breaths for Kane to bound down the stairs, followed by the short man.

"Max! Glad you came. You caught us just in time!" He ruffled my hair, giving me a noogie like we were old friends. Did he know Dad used to do that too? I squirmed away, but . . . it was nice someone actually *wanted* to see me. My lips quirked upward, even as Kane laughed, held up his hands. "Ah, too cool for that? I get it."

The short man beside him pressed his lips into a thin line but didn't speak.

Kane clapped my shoulder, gesturing at his ship. "Welcome to the *Enrapture*. Bit more impressive than Hames's trash heap, huh?"

"Mr. Hames has a Tracker Mark VI," I said automatically. Nerves got the better of me, and before I could stop myself, I tacked on, "with a Starkwil generator."

Kane rolled his eyes. "Faaancy."

The drawled word made my cheeks heat. Stupid. As if he'd care what Mr. Hames was flying. They obviously weren't friends, and I wasn't part of the *Calypso*'s crew anymore. So really, I shouldn't care either.

Before I could reply, though, Kaito's voice echoed on the intercom again. "Repeat. Max Belmont. Exit Hangar 13 immediately."

Kane raised his eyebrows. "You in trouble, kid?"

"Mom's coming," I said, cheeks heating again. "Did you call her, or—"

"Ah, didn't have the time, champ," he interrupted. "Been a bit busy preparing for launch. We're almost ready too, but I've got that box in the flight deck! If we're fast, I bet we can get you back outside the hangar before she even knows you're here."

They already knew I was here, but I needed that box. I nodded, and Kane grinned. "You're gonna love this." He led me up the staircase, opening the door with a flourish. "How about it, huh?"

It was . . . different from the *Calypso*. The hallway that welcomed us was expansive, stretching in either direction. The *Enrapture* was so big, it needed signs to direct people. "Escape pods, game room, ➡" and "Flight deck, mess hall, ⬅." Each of them was laser-printed in no-nonsense letters onto the metal walls. Everything was too clean, too white, devoid of any personality.

It reminded me of a hospital.

I shuddered, but Kane didn't notice. He seemed gleeful. "Pretty great, right?"

"Y-yeah. It's airtight," I replied hoarsely. The decivox case was heavy in my hands, and I wiped sweaty palms on my black uniform pants. Get the box, get out before Mom arrived. Simple. I didn't have to stay long.

"Follow me," Kane said. His strides were too long, and I was almost running to catch up. Crew members pacing the hallways pressed against the bulkhead walls, saluting as he passed. Like we were some kind of military vessel.

It was a little ridiculous. Mr. Hames never required us to salute.

But that doesn't matter anymore, I reminded myself. *And if you don't make it outside before Mom gets here, your life will be kids who hate you . . . and parent-enforced house arrest. Hurry up.*

After several agonizing minutes, Kane stopped at a closed door. He pressed his wrist against a locking mechanism, smiling when it clicked open. Some kind of computer chip embedded into his skin, maybe? Huh. Never seen anything like that before.

There were nine officers perched in stationary chairs, monitoring the main console. Conversation died when we entered, and someone called, "Captain on deck!"

I nearly laughed until I saw the serious expression on Kane's face. He pulled back his shoulders and said, authoritatively, "Status on departure."

"Crew is being recalled as we speak, sir. All systems online," a woman nearby replied, tapping away at the holoscreen before her. She didn't seem to notice me.

"Artificial gravity?"

"Engaging in three minutes. Launch in one."

Launch in one?

I shifted, scuffing the floor. A pit of unease settled in my stomach, souring like a bad vegetable. "Wait. Not yet. I have to get off the starship first."

"Maxion. On my ship, you don't speak until asked by a

superior officer." Kane's voice was hard now. He stared at me, cold and calculating, before saying, "Begin launch countdown."

"Aye, sir," a man to our left said, and activated the intercom. "Launch in fifty-five seconds. Report to stations."

He was kidnapping me.

Oh *stars*, he was kidnapping me. And none of the *Enrapture*'s crew even seemed to *care*.

Kane swept around his flight deck, coordinating the launch. Mom would get to Hangar 13 to find the doors closed again, this time with the airlock sealed, with me inside.

She was going to be so scared.

I was scared.

I needed to get out of here. Desperate, choking on fear, I spun toward the door. But it sealed shut before my eyes, and Kane said over my shoulder, "Max, I thought you liked starships. Aren't you excited to see how the *Enrapture* flies? It's the best starship your blackspace station will ever see."

"L-let me out," I pleaded.

He smirked, and cold fear settled in my gut. "I don't think so. One way or another, we're finding that star whale. But I'll tell you what. The sooner you show us where it is, the sooner we'll release you."

"But that wasn't the deal!"

Kane rubbed his mustache, smiling slightly. "Deal's changed. You'll get the box once you show us a star whale. I think that's fair."

"Launch imminent," the woman said.

Under my feet, the *Enrapture* began to shake.

And through the flight deck's windows, I saw Mom sprinting into the empty hangar. Saw her eyes land on the starship, saw her waving, shouting, eyes wild and panicked. The airlock doors slammed shut with her on the other side, and there was nothing she could do.

The *Enrapture* launched.

"No!" I screamed, dropping the decivox case to sprint past Kane. Maybe if I could wrench the controls from the navigators, I could get back to Azura. Back to Mom. Tears streamed down my face as I shouted again, "No! Take me back. Take me *home*!"

"Too late," Kane snarled, snatching me before I could reach his crew. And stars, he was strong. I thrashed in his grip, but he just yanked me along, stalking to the flight deck door. The ship swayed underneath us as it angled toward the asteroid belt. "And if you can't understand orders, you can't be in my flight deck."

He scooped up my decivox case, leaving the flight deck as pristine and empty as it'd been before. I sobbed as he stomped across the hall, pausing beside a closed metal door. Another wave of his wrist, and it opened into a tiny storage closet, barely bigger than the shed on the recreation level.

"Welcome to your quarters," he said, and tossed me inside. I landed with a thump that stole my breath, and while I was wheezing, he tossed the decivox's case onto me. It crashed into my side, and pain flared again. I gasped, curling into myself.

"Get comfortable," he said. "It's a long trip to the asteroid belt."

The door slammed shut, plunging me into darkness.

21

TALKING TO STAR WHALES

Nothing about the *Enrapture* was fast. If the time I was trapped in the cramped, dark storage closet was any indication, Kane would have been lucky to see a puff of purple smoke as Mr. Hames and the *Calypso* left him in the space dust.

I passed the time by playing soft tunes on the decivox. It wasn't loud enough that anyone could hear, but it felt better than screaming and pounding the door and crying for help. Something told me Kane's word was law on this starship. None of the crew would answer. None of them cared.

I was alone.

Tears pricked my eyes as the soft melody swirled around me. Dad's broken decivox still screeched, but I was playing so quietly it sounded more like cries of anguish than a malfunctioning instrument.

I'd been so *stupid*. Mr. Hames had warned me about Kane. He'd just been trying to help all this time. To find the star whales, to sweep us into adventure and maybe teach us something along the way. And I'd been so convinced this weird substitute teacher was the bad guy that I'd ignored the real villain.

India was right. I never should have reached out to Kane. Never should have been so desperate for a piece of Dad's past, not when the present was happening all around me. But it was *so* hard. Ever since Dad had died, it felt like I was barely surviving. Going through the motions of school, of pranks and jokes and laughter, while this massive storm cloud threatened to swallow me.

It wasn't fair. Why did Dad have to die? Of all the accidents in all the universe, why did one have to take *him*?

But I'd never found the answer to that, and it wouldn't help me now.

I wiped snot on my sleeve, lowering my hand from the decivox. The lack of music forced me to hear the *Enrapture*'s rumbling, the pounding footsteps of crew members who didn't care about the kid locked in the closet.

Mom cared. She'd seen me taken, and she wouldn't let that stand. The Azurans, my big edge-of-space family, were coming after me. And if Mr. Hames got involved, Kane would never be able to outrun them.

The thought filled me with confidence. I tightened my grip on the decivox, taking deep breaths until my trembling stopped, until my fear settled into cold determination. I'd messed up. But I couldn't change the past.

What I could change was my present.

So, okay. What were my options? I needed to stay near the *Enrapture*, or Mom would never find me. But . . . that didn't mean I had to stay *on* the *Enrapture*. He might not have realized it, but Kane had already made a mistake. He labeled everything on this massive ship, which meant I knew exactly where the escape pods were. If I could reach one of those, all I'd have to do was radio an SOS and wait.

My hand ghosted over my pant pocket, over the hydrodriver I carried everywhere. A smirk tilted my lips. Rhett had mocked me, but that "security blanket" might save my life. With it, I could definitely hot-wire an escape pod. I just had to *get* to one first.

And there was one more thing. A thrill raced through me as I dug into my jacket pocket, plucked out a certain marble. Stars, India thought of everything. A grin split my face as I rolled it between my fingers. Even without light, I imagined the swirl of blue and white on its smooth surface.

Kane wouldn't know what hit him.

I turned toward the door, staring hard at the inky black, bracing myself for a grand escape—when an eerie wail echoed through the starship's intercoms. It started soft at first, so quiet I thought it was a malfunctioning generator, but in seconds it bloomed into music, beautiful and terrifying.

No! They aren't supposed to be here!

Guilt choked me as I stuffed the smoke bomb into my jacket, snatched Dad's decivox again. I'd played it. I'd called them. But how could they have heard music barely loud enough for my ears?

Then again, how did they hear music at all? What if sound "couldn't travel in a vacuum" the same way living creatures "couldn't live in the vacuum of space"? Everything about them defied logic. Maybe a star whale's hearing was better than we could imagine.

Maybe I wasn't as alone as I'd thought.

I closed my eyes against the darkness and tried to decipher

what they were saying. The star whales were using higher notes, like a probing question.

Like . . . curiosity.

My hands found the decivox on instinct, and I concentrated hard. They didn't communicate with just anyone. They were talking to *me*, which meant maybe, just maybe, they could help. Smoke bomb or no, I'd rather not face Kane by myself.

I poured my desperation, my despair, into the next melody. This time, I didn't bother quieting the sound. I cranked the dials and played loud and long, recalling everything to this point: my classmates sneering at me, India rolling her eyes, Mr. Hames re-assuring me even though I didn't deserve it, Rhett shoving me to the floor, the pain of leaving the *Calypso* and my friends behind, the cautious hope of Kane's promise, the cold fear of his betrayal.

And then, the aloneness. That was trickiest, conveying the deepest, saddest part of my soul to these creatures. Spacing low notes far enough apart that they were like shuddering breaths. Wiggling my fingers into a soft vibrato that matched the dis-sonance of being locked in a dark room without my friends or family.

When I finally finished, tears leaked from my eyes, trailing down my cheeks in bitter accomplishment. If that didn't resonate with the whales, nothing would.

I counted to ten. Then twenty. Then a hundred. Silence. Maybe I'd imagined their calls, wished so desperately for the whales to find me that my brain created their song as a coping mechanism.

Of course, there was no way I imagined the footsteps outside the storage closet. My heart seized. Kane. Desperate, I fumbled for the smoke bomb, fumbled to get my plan back on track, but he was too fast. The door wrenched open, and his hand curled around my arm, yanking me into the corridor with little remorse. Dad's decivox clattered to the ground, and I yelped.

"That was a gorgeous melody," Kane said, smiling. I gasped as he twisted my arm, pushing me into the flight deck. Over his shoulder, he said to a crewmate, "Bring the instrument. Apparently, we're gonna need it."

He'd heard the whales. Of course he had; even Mr. Hames had heard their music before he saw them. I tried to escape his grasp, but Kane was bigger, stronger. He threw me to the ground as two crew members filed in behind us; one took position near the door while the other slid into the navigation seat. Beyond the windows, the dark shapes of asteroids blotted out thousands of distant stars. A few silver anemonium asteroids—whale excrement?—glittered amid the black.

The whales were nowhere to be seen.

"So, Max. You ready to help me find your friends?"

Did he mean the *Calypso* or the star whales? Either way, he was dreaming. I picked myself off the ground, silent. My head throbbed and my side ached and my arm twinged, but I wouldn't give him the satisfaction of knowing it.

Kane grabbed my chin, forcing my gaze upward. His beady eyes were dark and cold, so unlike Mr. Hames. His expression was nothing short of cruel. "There's no need to be nervous, Max. Just call back the whales and you can go home."

My eyes flicked to the other crew member, the one sitting at the navigation equipment. She was tapping buttons, monitoring scans. The one by the door crossed his arms stoically. This—this might be hard. One little smoke bomb didn't seem like enough now. The space was too big. There were too many people—too many obstacles.

With no other plan, I changed the subject.

"There's no box, is there? You don't have any of my dad's stuff."

"Ah, you finally found your brain." He retrieved my decivox from his lackey at the door, turning the instrument this way and that. Getting his grubby hands all over it.

I'd never been so offended.

"Give me that!"

Kane ignored me, shaking his head. "You know how long your dad was on the *Enrapture*, Max? Barely four weeks. Couldn't even manage a whole month."

Only four weeks? My heart sank. I hadn't wanted to face facts before, but India was right, wasn't she? Just because Kane had known Dad *didn't* mean they were friends. At least Mr. Hames was nice enough to admit he barely knew Dad.

Kane, meanwhile, crafted lie after lie, sucking me in like a black hole latching on to a starship.

Like a cannibalistic space siren preying on misbehaving kids.

"Why bother with this? Is it all for the money? Everything?"

Kane barked a laugh now, his mustache trembling with the sound. "Of course it's about the money, kid. *Milo* is an idealist. An optimist. But he got the *Enrapture* closer to a star whale than anyone, so when I heard he was on Azura, talkin' to Damian

Mendoza's kid, no less, I knew he'd found a lead." He smirked down at me. "But I have to hand it to you. All these years, and I never would've fathomed an *instrument* was the key to catching these things."

I clenched my fists. "They're not things. They're living creatures, with a real impact."

"And they're gonna make me very rich." His mustache curled, and he thrust the decivox into my hands. "Now, unless you want to see how inhabitable space can really be, you'll call them back."

No more stalling, apparently. But still, my fingers hovered over the hollow space of the decivox. I couldn't do it. I couldn't summon them into a trap.

"Go on," Kane growled.

"N-no." I lowered the instrument.

He took a step forward, but just as he raised his hand, just as I braced for a hit, a familiar wail echoed through the loudspeakers.

No.

Kane smiled so wide, he looked like a shark sighting his next meal. At the controls, his navigator gasped, and the goon behind me stiffened, but Kane seemed utterly calm. After all, he'd prepared for this moment.

"Guess they heard you the first time. Lucky break." Kane strolled to the plastiglass windows. The asteroids loomed, large and silent, but the star whales were still nowhere to be seen. "Jives, pinpoint that sound."

"Yes, sir," the woman at the computer said, and a few seconds later, the starship began a slow tilt. They peered out the windows, nearly pressing their noses to the plastiglass, waiting with bated breath for the whales to come into view.

It was kind of funny, in one of those "laugh so you don't cry" type ways.

I swallowed a desperate chuckle. My fingers curled around the smoke bomb, but before I could throw it, attempt an escape during the distraction, a hand dug into my neck. I yelped as my head throbbed sharply, a vivid reminder of when I'd made contact with the *Calypso*'s staircase. Suddenly weak-kneed, I barely heard the other crew member, the one guarding the door, announce, "Kid thinks something's funny, sir."

Kane faced me again, hands clasped behind his back. "What's the problem, Max? Something you'd like to share?"

"N-no," I choked, glaring.

His expression darkened. "In that case—"

That's when a flash of gold caught my eye, and dread nearly floored me. Because outside were not one, not two, but *three* star whales, drifting near the *Enrapture*, close, too close, like they thought this would help. Their music continued, louder now, a steady, reassuring stream of low notes that did nothing to calm my racing heart.

Kane read my face, spinning back to the windows. "They're here," he rasped, and Jives tapped the controls of the *Enrapture*, halting its slow spin. For a breath, everything was still.

The whales were going to be caught. This was the exact opposite of what I was supposed to be doing. It was great to imagine a grandiose escape at their side, but all I'd done was lead them into the jaws of a cruel, money-grubbing whaler. Desperate to buy them a few seconds, I laughed, despite the goon's hand gripping the back of my neck.

"You're dreaming, Kane. You got some kind of fancy whale soundtrack to get you in the mood for hunting?"

In the meantime, my fingers found the decivox, coaxing several high-pitched, desperate notes from its depth—*swim, flee, hurry!*—before the goon snatched the instrument.

The whales replied, just a few uneasy trills. My heart ached, though I set my jaw as Kane took the decivox from his lackey, examining it far more carefully this time. His eyes panned back to the asteroid belt. Stars, they were *so close* to the windows. Someone on this ship had to be seeing this.

Run, please!

"So, you are talking with them," Kane said, slowly. "Impressive. Where are they?"

"You'll never see them," I snarled, then whimpered as his goon tightened his grip on my neck.

Then Kane snapped, "Let him go."

Instantly, the lackey released me.

I staggered, desperate to catch my balance, but Kane loomed over me. "You said *I'll* never see them. Why? You kids didn't seem to have a problem with it."

I clamped my mouth shut, but he was a lot smarter than I'd given him credit for. He hummed contemplatively. "Is it a side effect of this space station? Radiation seeping through the hull, or some secret trick Azurans use to summon them . . . ?"

Any other moment, I'd have snorted at the idea of a "trick" to summon *whales*. What would it be? Some kind of crazy dance through the bulkhead windows? Or maybe, like, microptera screeching?

Or a decivox. Huh. Kind of did feel like a trick now.

I stayed silent as Kane circled me, puzzling through it. "Of course, Milo isn't from Azura. He hasn't been here long, has he? So it must be something special with you."

Now Kane knelt in front of me, squinting into my eyes. I glared back, defiantly. It didn't matter why we could see them and he couldn't, in my opinion. Knowing the reason wouldn't change the fact that he was as blind as Echo now.

But Kane was silent for a moment. Then his eyebrows rose. "Ah. It must be that simple: the class of children. That's why you can see them—but it doesn't explain Milo . . ."

Maybe if he thought he'd *never* see them, he'd drop me back on Azura and leave forever. I desperately blurted, "Mr. Hames couldn't see them either."

His hand cracked across my cheek, sending me sprawling. Pain hit, a fiery blast of anger that short-circuited my brain. He'd slapped me. And on the heels of that came a numbing certainty: unless something drastic happened, I was going to die on this starship.

And the worst part was, Mom wouldn't even know why.

"I don't appreciate lies," Kane said coldly. The snarky part of me longed to laugh and say, *Ironic*, but I couldn't form words. I needed help. Where was Mom? Where was Mr. Hames? How could I get out of this before the whales were captured—or before Kane decided I'd outlived my usefulness?

Kane meticulously handed the decivox back to his goon.

Then he knelt to my level as I picked myself off the ground, his eyes flashing. "I'm going to ask you one more time, Max. What did Hames do to see the star whales?"

And before I could answer, something huge slammed into the starship.

22

UNDER THE STAR WHALE'S SAIL

The entire ship pitched sideways, sending us all flying. Now or never.

I didn't think, didn't breathe, just covered my mouth and threw the bomb at Kane's feet. It burst in a truly spectacular fashion, and the flight deck filled with thick white smoke as I sprinted for the exit.

The goon at the door lunged for me, but I kicked and clawed and elbowed his face. He screamed and released me, and I took just a second to grab my dad's decivox—*my* decivox—before I skidded out of the flight deck and tore down the corridor.

Alarms blared, ratcheting my panic into truly paralyzing proportions. Crew members sprinted past, barely sparing me a glance as they shouted theories to each other. *We've hit an asteroid! There was an explosion in the engine room! The life support cut out!* But none of them were true.

I'd asked for help, and the star whales had obliged however they could.

Behind me, coughing hacks gave way to thundering footsteps and a fierce roar. "Find that kid!"

But I was already three corridors away, sprinting through an empty game room as the song of the star whales echoed through the loudspeakers in time with the alarms. Now they sounded angry, triumphant, like they were cheering me on from the vacuum of space.

I clutched Dad's decivox, digging for my hydrodriver as I skidded into the hallway with the escape pods. On a ship this size, there would be entire levels of escape pods—intergalactic law dictated one per two crew members, minimum. I chose one at random and dove inside. Like everything on this stupid ship, it was minimalistic at best: just a tiny orb outfitted with two thin seats and a control panel. I set the decivox in the passenger chair, facing the controls.

The totally dark controls. My eyes dropped on a tiny hole in the center of the console.

A thin box, identical to the one Kane had scanned outside the flight deck. It was illegal to lock escape pods, but that apparently hadn't stopped Kane from modifying these. Stars, how controlling *was* he? Supervising his crew all the way to the end? My heart caught in my throat, and I spun toward the open door leading back to the *Enrapture*.

Plan B, then. Lucky for me, Dad had taught me how to override a set of doors. And this model of escape pod was similar to Azuran mineships. Those could seal off the cockpit, jettison the pilot away from the ship's body in an emergency.

Which was the only reason Dad had made it back to Azura after the explosion. Had he felt like this, back then? Fueled by terror, injured and alone, facing imminent death?

Not the time. *Focus, or you'll never make it out alive.*

I drew a deep breath, boxed up my fear of Kane alongside devastating memories of Dad, calming my mind to focus on the task at hand. I needed the override, a small panel near the door—*there*! Gnawing on my lower lip, I powered on my hydrodriver and popped off the panel.

Footsteps pounded near the end of the hallway. "He went this way!"

Kane's response was more of a snarl. *"Find him.* Bring him to me!"

Stars. I swallowed hard, pressing myself further against the curved wall of the escape pod. They didn't know where I was . . . not yet. There were ten escape pods on this level, and I could be in any of them. *Use that time. Close this door!* My hydrodriver whirred softly beneath the urgent undertones of the star whales. Another massive slam rocked the *Enrapture*, and more alarms blared.

A third voice: "Captain, we're under attack. We shouldn't be wasting time—"

Kane's footsteps stopped, and then a gasping sound filled the hallway, barely audible beyond the blaring alarms and the whales' songs.

Was he *choking* his crew member?

A thump, a shuddering gasp, and Kane hissed, "Anyone else?"

No response.

"Don't *ever* tell me how to captain my starship," he said, and the murmurs of *"Yes, sir"* sounded partly horrified, but mostly resigned. Maybe his flight deck crew *had* wanted to help me. Maybe they were just too scared to try.

I set my jaw. My time was measured in seconds now.

This panel wasn't like the gnarled mess of wires we dealt with on Azura. This one had a simple fan inside, a secondary power source that could activate everything remotely. In fact, it kind of reminded me of Mr. Keller's hertz-rated infibrillator. And lucky me, I'd just fixed that. I swapped my hydrodriver's tip out for the electrical prong used to shock a charge into electronics.

"There he is—"

The hydrodriver sparked, and I shoved the metal piece against the fan's mechanisms. It glowed white and began to spin, and just as Kane sprinted into view, the escape pod's door slammed shut.

I was shaking so hard, the hydrodriver clattered to the floor. But the door was closed. Locked from the inside. Kane couldn't reach me now, and he knew it. And yet, when I half expected him to lose his temper, to beat on the glass like a caged animal, instead he just narrowed his eyes in final warning.

A chill raced up my spine. That look seemed like a promise. Like even though I'd escaped, I still wasn't getting out of this alive.

Trembling, I staggered backward to the control panel, which was glowing to life thanks to the fan's power. My eyes never left Kane's.

The starship lurched again, and he regained his balance long enough to hold my gaze one last time. Then he stalked out of sight.

Somehow, that was scarier.

I wasted no time slamming the release button to eject the

pod. The pod jettisoned into the thick of the asteroid belt. My heart thrummed and my head pounded; sweat poured down my face, and I felt close to tears.

But I was free.

And then I saw the star whales properly.

Two were focused on destroying the *Enrapture* one violent pounding at a time. They moved in slow motion, but their bulk was enough to dent the starship's hull with every hit, crippling its defenses. In direct contrast to the *Calypso*, the *Enrapture* had guns, hulking masses that must have been tucked inside the roof while it was docked on Azura. But for all its armature, the crew had no idea what to aim at.

They couldn't see what was attacking.

I nearly laughed, until I realized the third whale had set its sights on me. It approached with ferocity, and panic clouded my mind. It didn't know who I was! It probably thought I was Kane, abandoning a sinking starship.

I fumbled for my decivox, playing a few desperate notes. Trying to convey my happiness at escaping, tinged with the fear of what I'd left behind.

The third whale slowed, circling me from above. But it didn't attack.

Instead, its reply was soothing, harmonious.

Relief hit me like a stair to the head. It worked. Thanks to them, I'd gotten away. I was *safe*. But then I glanced back at the *Enrapture*, realized its guns had swiveled in a different direction.

They couldn't see the whales, but they saw me.

Kane's unspoken promise echoed in my mind.

My breath hitched as I frantically tapped the controls. But there was nowhere to go. Escape pods weren't designed for finesse or speed. I wouldn't be able to maneuver through the belt without slamming into an asteroid. I wouldn't escape his guns.

I was going to die here.

And just as that thought cemented into my mind, the whale descended. Its glimmering golden sails—they really did look like fluid, fabric solar panels—settled over my escape pod like a blanket. Through the fade and shimmer of the sails, I watched the *Enrapture*'s guns rise, lower, spin. Like they'd lost sight of me.

Like I'd vanished.

I laughed then, grinning widely as I grabbed my decivox and played a few notes of raw gratitude. Kane was so far from childlike wonder, he'd *never* see the star whales. And if today was any indication, his crew wouldn't either.

The other whales continued their assault on the *Enrapture*. The lights went out, the hull caved inward, and the ship hissed oxygen. Several more escape pods launched, and I gulped. His crew was getting away. *Kane* might be getting away. I wanted everyone safe, but the thought of that man free, lurking outside Azura, was petrifying.

The star whale protecting me hummed again, a low, inquisitive sound that ended on an upswing. A kind of "oh, look over there" noise. I spun away from the *Enrapture*'s demise to see two more whales . . . leading the *Calypso* through the asteroid belt.

"Airtight!" I shouted, flashing the whale a thumbs-up before remembering it wouldn't have a clue what that was. Instead, I grabbed the decivox, twirled my fingers into a tune of elation. Triumph.

It responded in kind, and its fin nudged me toward the *Calypso*, the same way it nudged aside the asteroids. Although the asteroids didn't care about the force of that push—meanwhile, I lurched toward the plastiglass, nearly smacked my head against the console. My fingers scrabbled for the harness, buckling it just as the whale pushed the escape pod again.

Still, you wouldn't hear me complaining.

Through the windows, across a vast space, Mr. Hames and my class waved frantically at me. I waved back, swallowing past the sudden lump in my throat. Even as Mr. Hames guided his starship beside my pod, unlocked the receptacle in the engine room, and sucked me in, I couldn't believe it.

I was back on the *Calypso*, and I'd never been so happy.

The escape pod clicked into place, the pressure equalized, and then India thumped against the cold plastiglass of the escape pod. She was the only one there, panting slightly like she'd just sprinted for her life.

"Open the door," she mouthed, her eyes alight.

Stars, I hadn't even realized how much I missed her. I scrambled to oblige, and the door hissed open and I fell on top of her—and then we were laughing and hugging, and everything was suddenly okay.

"I'm sorry," I practically chanted as I gripped her. "I'm sorry. I'm sorry. I messed up."

"I know," she replied. I elbowed her, and she stuck her tongue out at me, then helped me stand. "This was so stupid, Max. When I said I wanted to travel, I thought we'd do it together. You and me."

"What about your mom?"

Her cheeks darkened. "I made that up. If she wanted to travel, she'd have left with my dad. But she's always loved Azura." After a moment, India scuffed the floor with her boot. "I mean, I guess I do too."

I poked her shoulder. "As awesome as Azura is, we'd never have seen *them* if we didn't explore." I jerked a thumb at the engine room's windows, at the star whales circling our ship. She grinned at me, and I hugged her again. As an afterthought, I said, "Oh, I owe you a smoke bomb."

"What?"

Then Mr. Hames slid down the ladder, followed by the rest of our class, minus Louisa . . . and Arsenio. Probably *one* of the Flight Deckers needed to be up top monitoring things. Maybe Arsenio was trying to help her—or, more likely, I'd finally scared him off.

But before I could ask, Mr. Hames took my shoulders, shaking them like it had been weeks instead of hours. "Max. Thank the stars!"

I didn't even scoff when he ruffled my hair. To be honest, it kind of felt like weeks to me too.

I became acutely aware of everyone staring. Most of them seemed happy, relieved, but Tarynn and Rhett looked embarrassed. They wouldn't quite look at me, stood close enough to show support without invading my space.

I was kind of grateful for that.

Still, I made a point to meet their gazes in turn and offered a smile. Not a pained one, a fake one, an "I'm pretending we're fine because of what happened, but this will come up later" one. No, the smile I offered was one of humility and defeat.

You messed up, it said. *But so did I.*

Tarynn and Rhett exchanged a glance, and Tarynn stepped forward, wrapping me in a hug. "Welcome back, Max." Then her tone hardened. "Don't try that again, or I'll have to report you."

I rolled my eyes as India pushed her away.

But the word "report" reminded me of the most pressing matter, and I spun back to Mr. Hames. "Wait! Kane's getting away. The star whales destroyed his ship, but—"

"Oh, trust me. Your mother is already bringing the entirety of Azura's police force."

I stiffened, eyebrows shooting into my messy hair. "Wait. You *did* call her?"

"After you abandoned my starship seconds before launch and almost got trapped in an airlock? Of course I called her," Mr. Hames said, rolling his eyes. "Childlike wonder or not, I'm still the responsible one here."

"Hey!" Tarynn exclaimed, indignant.

My mind spun. "So, she knows about this expedition? Aren't you going to get in trouble?"

Mr. Hames rubbed his arm. "There's a good chance Kane won't be the only one arrested today."

"We can talk to our uncle," Nashira offered.

"I mean, you can try. But this is basically kidnapping, in

their eyes. Azura has laws for a reason," Tarynn said, reluctant to meet Mr. Hames's gaze.

Our teacher forced a bright tone. "Well, if nothing else, I'll be staying on Azura longer than expected."

Sure. In a jail cell.

Guilt settled like a hot lump in my chest. He'd known this was a possibility, but with the chaos of the other whalers, he might have gotten away with it . . . if not for me.

But before I could say something, he met my gaze knowingly. "Max. None of this is your fault. You know what is? Getting me to see these majestic creatures again. That's all I've wanted since that night on the refugee ship, and it wouldn't have happened without your music. Thank you."

India nudged me. I blushed, cheeks warming as my eyes flicked to the Starkwil generator, my classmates, the *Calypso*'s engine room.

Maybe being at fault wasn't always a bad thing.

A *beep* echoed through the ship's intercom, followed by Louisa's apprehensive voice. "Um, Nashira? M-Ms. Belmont is pinging us. What should I do?"

Nashira flinched, spinning toward Mr. Hames. "That didn't last long."

"I never expected it to," he sighed. "Louisa, who's on that call?"

A moment of silence. Then:

"Ms. Belmont, and the mayor. And—the chief of police."

23

THE SECRETS OF AZURA

Mr. Hames rubbed his face. "Okay, let's get this over with. I'll be up in a moment, Louisa." He paused, seizing one last glance at the star whales. They sang to each other, having whole conversations as their golden sails shimmered over the *Calypso*. Mr. Hames cleared his throat and glanced back at me. "Ah, Max, isn't there one more thing you need to do?"

India ducked into the escape pod, resurfacing with my broken, perfect decivox. "Yeah, you should have seen us trying to send the star whales away. Apparently we all suck at playing that instrument. I think they thought we were throwing a temper tantrum."

"Or a rock concert," Nashira joked as she hauled herself up the ladder. Tarynn gulped, surveying the thin opening, but clenched her eyes shut and followed. Her mom was apparently waiting, after all.

"Ah, Mr. Hames?" Louisa said over the intercom. "They're . . . asking for urgency."

She made it seem like "asking" wasn't the right word.

"Quickly, Max." Our teacher gestured at the decivox, then followed them up the ladder, out of sight. The rest of the class trickled up too, until it was just India and me.

I wasted no time starting to play. It just took a few minutes, desperately weaving a narrative that included our excitement on finding them, followed by the greed and violence of Kane's desires to hunt them, capture them. I tried to imagine a happier place, somewhere else they could live and sing with no restrictions until it was safe to return. *Go there. Here isn't great right now.*

We held our breaths as the whales considered my song.

And then, one by one, they turned to leave, swimming away from the asteroid belt, away from Azura, away from *us*.

Hopefully not forever . . . but if it was, Azura would manage. After all, it was the people that made somewhere great, not their export.

"Wow. You made that look really easy," India drawled. Pride tinged her voice.

"I have to go help Mr. Hames," I said, pushing the decivox into her hands. "But—we'll talk soon?"

"There's not much more to say." India grinned.

I grinned back, relishing our old normal, before climbing the ladder to the main deck, then scaling the spiral staircase in a few steps. The rest of the class lingered at the base of the flight deck's ladder, eavesdropping—everyone except Arsenio.

I skidded to a stop at the open medbay door, glancing inside.

He was staring numbly at his medical game, tapping absently on the holographic image instead of twisting and turning it, squinting like usual.

Mom was waiting, but, well, I'd been a bad friend for long enough. I ducked into the medbay, rubbing the back of my head. It felt swollen, and the dried blood was crusty beneath my fingers.

My voice was hesitant, at best. "Um . . . h-hey, Arsenio. After I talk with my mom, do you think I can get some help?"

He spun toward me, eyes widening. "You *want* my help?"

"I shouldn't need more than a wet cloth, probably? But I think I might have a concussion."

I hoped he could see that for what it was: a peace offering, spoken in his language.

Arsenio stared at me for a beat, as if gauging my sincerity. Then a massive smile split his face, and he immediately procured bandages and antiseptic. "I'll be here! Whatever you need, Max."

I smiled, moved to step back into the hallway but paused. My gaze met his again. "T-thanks. For everything. I was mad—about your mom, and my dad. But it wasn't fair to put that on you."

Arsenio's hands lowered, and his head drooped. "I'm really sorry she couldn't save him, Max. I don't blame you for anything."

"I do," I mumbled. Then I stepped forward and hugged him, just like we used to when we were younger. Before everything soured. It was just a quick embrace, but when I pulled back, Arsenio was beaming brighter than the sun.

"I want to be friends again," I said. "It just—might take me some time. Is that okay?"

Arsenio nodded emphatically. "I'll be here. You know. When you want help."

"Max! We need you," India called, poking her head into the medbay. She and Arsenio shared a grin as I backed out of his area.

"I'll be back," I promised.

Arsenio flashed me a thumbs-up, and suddenly we were

okay too. Relief spread through me as I trailed after India, as the crowd at the base of the ladder parted to allow me upstairs. Apparently, they were prioritizing the kids whose relatives were on this holocall: me, Tarynn, and Nashira. Louisa was hovering at the base, nose-deep in her holopad, pretending not to hear the argument above. She never liked conflict much.

But she did offer me a brief pat on the shoulder as I climbed upstairs.

Into a massacre, apparently. Nashira and Tarynn were pressed against the back wall, while a larger-than-life hologram of Mayor Zhang projected into the center of the flight deck. Mr. Hames shrank under her ire.

"—taking *our* children into the asteroid belt—without permission, no less! When I approved the field study program, I never *imagined* you'd use it for child labor, and then kidnapping. You have violated so many of our laws—"

"But Mom—" Tarynn started.

"*Don't* interrupt me, young lady."

"Where's Max?" my mom's desperate voice filtered in from the side, and her holographic head floated over Mayor Zhang's shoulder. "You said you found him. Is he on board your ship?"

"I'm here! Mom, I'm fine," I said, waving at the camera over the wide windows so they could see I was okay.

Mayor Zhang's image stepped out of the picture, allowing my mother's form to take her place. Mom looked immensely relieved, her sharp eyes scouring me for signs of injury. "Thank the *stars*. Are you hurt, Max? What on Azura propelled you into that man's ship?"

Well, that was an argument for another time. I redirected the conversation. "It doesn't matter. His crew is getting away—"

"How many crew members does he have?" another, deeper voice demanded. Now Mom stepped aside to allow Nashira and Louisa's uncle into the hologram. He was a tall, foreboding man wearing a police uniform with stripes pinned to the lapel.

"His crew complement's a hundred," I replied quickly. "But they're all under Kane's control. He choked one of them for questioning him, so I'm not sure how many of them are criminals."

"Who's Kane?" The chief tugged a holopad from the recesses of his jacket, tapping some notes.

I jerked a thumb at the windows. "The captain. Buzz cut, blond mustache. I'm sure he's in one of those escape pods."

"That ship is destroyed. What *happened*? Max, are you sure you're all right?" Mom's panicked voice was back.

Mr. Hames glanced at me, expression concerned now. I gingerly touched the back of my head, where I'd been bleeding a few hours ago. "Thanks to Mr. Hames. That's what I'm saying. You guys are mad at the wrong guy."

"Yeah. He didn't kidnap us. We *asked* to come with him," Nashira said.

A soft murmur of agreement made me peek down the ladder, only to see our classmates still congregating, still eavesdropping. Nosy bunch.

Then again, Azurans always were.

"One rescue doesn't pardon the fact that he took six other children—including my *nieces*—on a joyride. Milo Hames.

Return your starship to Azura immediately." The tone in Nashira's uncle's voice left no room for argument.

Mr. Hames hung his head. "Yes, sir. Of course."

But now Mom stepped back into the picture, her holographic face puzzled. "Wait a moment, Amir. None of this explains *why* they went to the asteroid belt. And isn't it convenient timing, considering the influx of visitors we've had in the last few days?"

I flinched. Of course Mom had figured it out.

"Max. What was your class doing out here? What did Kane want with you?"

Mr. Hames watched me, carefully, silently. He wasn't going to intervene. I had a chance to tell Mom the truth about the star whales. But spilling secrets got me into this mess in the first place.

I wouldn't make the same mistake twice.

I drew a ragged breath. "I-I can't tell you. I'm sorry, Mom."

And then the star whales' song echoed through our ships, one final goodbye.

We couldn't see them from this angle, but their music rang loud and clear on our intercom, colossal, deafening, yet gorgeous and sad and uplifting all at once. It vibrated the whole starship, and based on how Mom staggered, they'd heard it too.

Her eyes widened. "W-was that . . . a star whale?"

Hang on.

What?

"You *know* about them?" Mr. Hames yelped. Then he paused, rubbed his forehead, sounding exasperated. "Wait, wait. Damian. Of course, he told you."

But Mom wasn't listening. She'd turned to confer with Mayor

Zhang and Chief Amir. Before any of us could reply, though, she was back, eyes narrowed on Mr. Hames. "So you're a whaler. Which means those people clogging our corridors are whalers too. We have to act fast."

"Act fast?" I repeated dumbly.

"Milo. Who did you tell?"

Mr. Hames looked offended now. "No one."

Mom scowled. "You obviously told *someone*, or whalers wouldn't have infested Azura. These creatures are under our protection. If the whole galaxy knows they're here, we need to know." Her expression softened somewhat. "Milo, please."

"Camille, I didn't *tell* anyone."

"I did," I admitted, wincing. "I told Kane, and the information leaked. But they don't know *where* the whales are, or that they're hidden from most adults. All they know is a rumor that someone saw the star whales nearby."

"And Max just sent the whales away. So they're safe. It's over." Mr. Hames gestured to the empty space between our starships, but by Mom's confused expression, she couldn't see the whales—or absence of them—at all.

I knew Mr. Hames was special, weird enough to remember being a kid, but—in the last few minutes, I'd really hoped Mom could see them too. Apparently, our teacher was something of a rarity all on his own.

Mayor Zhang muscled her way into the hologram again, eyebrows brushing her perfectly cut bangs. "I'm sorry. Did you just say he *sent* them away?"

"Max talks to star whales through his decivox," Nashira said, shooting me a grin.

Mayor Zhang's jaw dropped. "W-what? Camille, did Damian—"

I held my breath, but offscreen, Mom sounded just as perplexed. "No. I mean, he had a theory. But as far as I knew, it never worked. That's why he stopped playing when Max was just a baby."

But that meant I was the only one who could communicate with them. Mom and Dad and the others knew they existed, but apparently none of *them* opened a dialogue with the star whales . . . not even Dad.

Mom took position in the hologram, drawing a deep breath. I could see her compartmentalizing, prioritizing the whales over the discussions we clearly needed to have. Her voice was steady, soothing. "Max, honey, are you sure the whales aren't here anymore?"

"*None* of you can see them?" Mr. Hames asked, incredulous.

Mom shook her head. "Not anymore. They don't like adults."

They'd liked Dad, though. But of course they would; Dad was a lot like Mr. Hames, delighted by the wonders of life. I thought back to Dad's pranks of hacking hangar doors. Winning Mom a stuffed animal just to see her smile. Coaxing me through the process of fixing something, elbow-deep in machine parts and grease as he cheered me on.

Mom wasn't like that, but she loved that part of him. Dad was special. And now, Mr. Hames was special. I wondered if she felt envious, unjustly cheated, knowing our teacher could see what she couldn't. It seemed that way when she added, darkly, "And we can't risk another whaler getting lucky."

Stars, she acted like our teacher was stalking the whales with a giant harpoon gun, which wasn't fair. I crossed my arms. "Come on, Mom. Mr. Hames had plenty of opportunities to catch a star whale, but he didn't. He isn't after the government grant."

Chief Amir's gruff voice filtered through the comms. "A whaler, not hunting for digits? Sure."

"It's true," Louisa said, meekly poking her head through the hole in the floor.

Nashira joined her sister. "Yeah. He's one of the good guys. He really wants to protect the star whales."

"Frankly, he's been more honest about it than *you* three have," Tarynn added haughtily. Mutters of agreement echoed.

Mr. Hames ignored us, holding Mom's gaze. "I'm in the business of exploration and discovery, Camille. Let me help. Now that the star whales have left, I can get rid of the whalers. Everything will be fine."

Mom surveyed him, one of those gazes that seemed to strip every layer of who Mr. Hames was, peeling back lies and cover stories to find the truth. Her gaze slid to me next, but this time I had nothing to hide. I stood tall, defiant. I'd made mistakes, but trusting Mr. Hames wasn't one of them.

Eventually, she sighed. "What did you have in mind?"

"Camille!"

"We don't have a choice," Mom said sharply. "What's your alternative, Kyrene? Blast the *Calypso* into the asteroids? Our *kids* are on his ship."

Mr. Hames straightened, indignant. "Now, that's a bit extreme. No matter what you decide to do with me, I'll get the kids home safe. That's my job."

"Not for long," Chief Amir growled.

Mom pinched the bridge of her nose. "Enough, Amir. Like it or not, we have to face facts. At any point during this conversation, Milo could have called the whalers. But no one else is here, which means he's telling the truth." When none of them argued, she folded her arms. "So, I want to know your plan, Milo. How are you going to get the whalers off Azura?"

Mr. Hames grinned, jerking a thumb at the escape pods drifting through space. "Simple redirection."

EPILOGUE

Turned out, whalers were just as susceptible to rumors as Azurans were. All it took was a few well-planted conversations about Kane's arrest and an increase of police involvement in the hangar level, and the whalers decided Azura wasn't worth the trouble. Their mass exodus left the corridors blissfully empty, and things got back to normal.

Well, most things.

About a week after we sent the star whales away, Mom and I paused outside Hangar 42. Through the open airlock doors, the *Calypso* loomed dark and silent. It felt *wrong*, seeing it unused like this. I rubbed my arm, hesitating.

Mom double-checked her holopad, then glanced at me. "You okay, honey?"

"Are you sure he's expecting us?"

Before she could answer, a cheery shout caught our attention. "Oh! You're early. Welcome!" Mr. Hames was carrying a huge box, and all we could see was a tuft of his red hair. He staggered down the *Calypso*'s steps, gasping for breath.

"Oh stars," Mom said, and hurried over to help.

Too little, too late, because Mr. Hames missed a step and careened headlong into her. She managed to catch him, but the box crashed to the floor. What looked like pink potting soil spilled from one corner, and Mr. Hames yelped, pushing us both several feet from it.

"It's fine, it's fine! Don't touch it. It shouldn't hurt anything, but . . . stand over here just to be safe." He laughed sheepishly.

Mom narrowed her eyes, but her lips tilted upward. "Do I want to know what that is?"

"It's certainly not alive, I can promise that," Mr. Hames said, too quickly.

I snickered.

Mom heaved a sigh and turned the holopad toward him. The golden glow illuminated his eyes, alight with excitement, and he said, "Oh! Is—is this my lease?"

"The mayor just needs your thumbprint. The apartment's small, but it should suffice, provided you don't fill it with . . . illicit items." Her gaze dropped to the pink soil. Might have been my imagination, but it sure looked like it was creeping across the floor.

Mr. Hames nudged it back into the box with the toe of his boot. "Of course, of course. I'm meticulously kid-proofing my starship."

"So don't go near your apartment, is what you're saying," I said with a wicked grin.

Mom shot me an exasperated look and waited while Mr. Hames signed the holopad. She sent the documents to Mayor Zhang, then tucked the thin device into her back pocket. "Well, that's one thing settled. Now all you need is your teaching license, and you're set as a proper Azuran." Her gaze hardened. "And no more unsanctioned trips. Right?"

"Right," he replied, deadly serious. "So no one knows about—?"

"Your excursions?" Mom glanced over her shoulder, but we were alone in the hangar. "The star whales aren't common knowledge, Milo. We just can't trust an entire space station to keep that secret. I hadn't even expected the kids to find out, but what's done is done."

I scuffed the floor, jaw clenched. Luckily, Kane wasn't in a position to reveal the truth, and the other whalers were gone, but I still felt guilty about what I'd done.

Mr. Hames put a hand on my shoulder, offering a broad smile. "We won't tell anyone. Right, Max?"

"Yeah. Not that it matters, anyway; the whales all left," I said with a shrug. I'd made amends, but I still felt guilty about everything. "We'll be lucky if Azura has anemonium to mine in a year."

We'd filled them in on our theory about the anemonium asteroids, but Dad had figured it out decades ago. Even now, Mom smiled knowingly, turning her gaze to the stars beyond the airlock. "Oh, I wouldn't be so certain about that. This stretch of the asteroid belt is an optimal place to live, where their solar sails can collect enough light to survive without being overheated. You sent them away for a bit, but whales always migrate home."

Excitement raced through me. "Really?"

Mom laughed. "Stars, Max, you really are just like your father."

Mr. Hames coughed into his hand, then jerked a thumb at the fallen box. "I'd better take care of this. Let me know if either of you gets a fever, hallucinations . . . bulbous feet . . . purple splotches on your pinky fingers . . ." He trailed off, laughing nervously at our horror. "Just kidding."

He didn't sound like he was kidding.

After hasty goodbyes, Mom towed me out of the hangar. We didn't talk until we got back to our apartment, until the front door was closed and I was rummaging around for a snack and Mom plopped onto the couch.

Her eyes drifted to the holographic pictures on the wall, the ones of me as a baby, of her and Dad at their wedding, of our family portraits. I dropped to the floor beside her, staring at the carpet, munching on carrot sticks.

And finally, I was brave enough to bring it up.

"Why didn't you tell me about the star whales?"

She picked up a pillow, rearranging herself against the opposite armrest of the couch. The soft blue pillow had a string loose, and she absently plucked at it. "I wanted to, Max. But—I was scared."

Scared? How could she be scared of those magnificent creatures?

"Why?"

Mom closed her eyes. "Your father and I were ten years old when we saw our first star whale. I wanted to stay on Azura, coordinate with Kyrene and Amir and the others who saw it too. Without the whales, Azura would fall to ruin . . . but more than that, they're special. We had to keep their secret. But for all that I wanted to stay here, your dad wanted to leave."

Oh. It had never occurred to me that Mom and I had something like this in common—our best friend reaching for the stars, while we kept our feet planted on a space station.

"Is that why he joined the *Enrapture*?"

"Yeah." She shook her head. "When we were sixteen, a whaler showed up asking questions. Damian was sure others would follow, so he took a preemptive strike. Joined their crew to 'redirect from the inside.'" She laughed hollowly. "It was the biggest fight we ever had, but he went anyway. And even though he came back, I was scared if I mentioned it, you might do the same thing."

I laughed. What a crazy idea. "Leaving Azura? Mom, I'm twelve. Where would I go?"

"You're a pretty resourceful kid," she replied, almost proud now. "And you won't be twelve forever."

She had a point there.

Mom sighed. "I should have paid more attention, Max. To what was happening with you, to how you were coping. I was so overwhelmed with grief that I forgot *you* lost someone too. Milo told me how desperate you were to reconnect with your father, and . . . t-that's my fault. When you had questions about who he was, I should have been your first stop."

"I didn't want to make you cry," I whispered.

"Honey, we lost a third of our family. Crying is healthy." Mom patted the space on the couch beside her, and I abandoned the carrots to scoot onto the cushion. She curled me into her side, holding me close.

My eyes burned. "I miss him. So much."

"I do too." Her voice wobbled. "But he's always with us. You can see him every time you look outside."

She gestured to the windows, to the plenitude of stars moving slowly beyond Azura. They were merely pinpricks, but every single one could be a memory of how he smiled, how he laughed, how he lived. I'd never thought about it like that before, but it was nice, remembering him when I saw the stars.

Mom cleared her throat, ruffling my hair. "Did you know Milo was part of the cleanup crew for the *Enrapture*? He found something for you." She kissed my forehead, then climbed off the couch to retrieve a tiny brown package from one of the kitchen drawers. She took her seat again, hugging the pillow as I ripped off the brown packaging. Inside was a thin leather pouch stamped with *Skee's Music Emporium*.

The best instrument repair shop in the Fifth Star System.

With trembling fingers, I unfastened the button, lifting the cover of the repair kit. There were five tools of all shapes and sizes, their wooden handles worn from use. One looked like a screwdriver that would perfectly tighten the metal rod on Dad's decivox.

My breath caught.

"You can fix your decivox now, right? Milo thought it would help. Said he found it under your dad's old bunk."

"Y-yeah," I said, not trusting myself to say more.

Mom smiled. "I didn't know you were so skilled with that instrument, Max. I'm not trying to push you toward engineering, if that isn't what you want to do. You have to follow your dreams."

My dreams? I used to want to play the decivox, but that was

before I fixed a Starkwil slipstream generator. Now it seemed silly to choose between two things I truly enjoyed.

"Can't I do both?"

Surprised, Mom laughed. "What a novel concept. Now, when are you going to play for me?" She lowered her voice to a conspiratorial whisper. "I hear you can summon whales in space."

I rolled my eyes, but pride swept through me anyway. "Wait right here!"

It only took me a few minutes to reattach the metal rod with my new repair kit, only took a breath to test the tuning and hear Dad's decivox's true sound for the first time. It was *magnificent*, and the melody of it settled into my bones, bringing me back to the glory of those whales, swimming in space.

With memories of Dad swirling in my mind, and Mom listening from the couch, I played. And somewhere out in space, I knew the star whales were listening.

ACKNOWLEDGMENTS

I spent a week paralyzed by indecision about how to write these acknowledgments, in desperate fear of leaving out someone vitally important. Because honestly, so many amazing and encouraging people have helped me get to this point. Writing is inherently a lonely task, but the people who rally around you, who support you, who teach you—they're the ones who show you what success truly means.

A remarkable thanks to Mari for plucking this book out of her submissions pile and giving it—and me—a chance. The staff at Jolly Fish Press have been incredible, and I'm so lucky to work with you all. Special *huge* thanks to Sarah for designing the cover of my dreams, and to Rebecca for illustrating it to perfection. (I definitely haven't framed it to admire day and night. Nope.) And a big thanks to Jake, the book designer. The little details on every chapter page made my jaw drop!

The absolute biggest YOU'RE AMAZING to my literary agent, Kaitlyn. I can't express how grateful I am that you've been guiding my career, editing my work, and offering tips and tricks and encouragement in a business of rejection. It really means everything to me. You are, as always, a rock star!

Another massive thank-you to my family: my parents, my sister, my grandparents, my aunts and uncles and cousins. Writing is easy, but publishing is hard, and your support over the years has been invaluable. I love you guys so much! Special shout-out to Gaga and Pap for keeping a copy of *Note to Self*—my terrible self-published ghost story—on their coffee table for over a decade. You always knew I could do it. ♥

To my dear friends, the ladies who formed my critique groups: you guys are incredible. Without your feedback, *Star Whales* wouldn't have been more than an unpolished, horrendous idea in my head. You made me the writer I am today.

A huge thanks to the National Novel Writing Month community in Phoenix. All the write-ins, the critique sessions, the editing partners, the friendships, the memories . . . meeting like-minded people and watching everyone grow has been so inspiring. To many more years of success for all of us!

And finally, to my career as a flight attendant. Thank you, Southwest Airlines, for giving me a job that lets me write four days a week without going broke, and for all our CoHearts who have encouraged me along the way.

To any budding writers out there hoping to publish their own work, never *ever* give up! *Star Whales* was my fourteenth novel, and it was a long road to get here. You never know when that "yes" is around the corner. Keep writing, for all of us; we need your novel!

ABOUT THE AUTHOR

The wild Rebecca Thorne can be found in her natural habitat: the local coffee shop. She is rarely more than an arm's length from her laptop and her "Becky's" coffee mug. When not in pursuit of caffeine, she prefers to relax with her two dogs, ensconced in her butt-cloud beanbag sofa. She might have been the flight attendant cracking puns on your last Southwest flight . . . or she might have been trying not to melt in the Arizona heat while you traveled the country.

Rebecca has been writing since she was eleven years old and has never cared to leave her young protagonists. Though she prefers fantasy and science fiction, she's dabbled in every genre under the middle grade umbrella.